Molly wondered if she was the first girl to ever fall in love in a riptide. Okay, to say that she had fallen in love was perhaps too strong a statement. But she had fallen into something more significant than just his arms. They surged up with the swell, and he pulled her to him a little tighter.

"Well, thank you for saving my life and all. I really do appreciate it," she said.

They were washed four hundred more yards south before there was a break in the wave pattern and they finally emerged out of the surge of swiftly flowing water.

Leaving him to follow his own pipe dream, Molly tumbled to shore on the crest of a three-footer. Only five minutes before, she had longed to touch solid ground. But as she trudged through the wet sand, she felt oddly sad to be leaving the water. She turned and shaded her eyes just in time to see him catch the best wave of the day, a spurt of perfection. Her breath quickened as she watched how beautifully he surfed the break, a lone surfer on a long, endless ride.

And she couldn't help thinking to herself that falling in love was a lot like being in a rip. You don't know you're in it until it's too late.

ALSO BY KAROL ANN HOEFFNER

All You've Got

SURF ED.

KAROL ANN HOEFFNER

SIMON PULSE
NEW YORK | LONDON | TORONTO | SYDNEY

SIMON PULSE

An imprint of Simon & Schuster Children's Publishing Division
1230 Avenue of the Americas, New York, NY 10020
Copyright © 2007 by Karol Ann Hoeffner
All rights reserved, including the right of reproduction
in whole or in part in any form.
SIMON PULSE and colophon are trademarks of
Simon & Schuster, Inc.
Designed by Steve Kennedy
The text of this book was set in Jante Antiqua.
Manufactured in the United States of America
First Simon Pulse edition May 2007
2 4 6 8 10 9 7 5 3 1
Library of Congress Control Number 2007923284
ISBN-13: 978-1-4169-3970-2
ISBN-10: 1-4169-3970-9

*To the waterman who showed me the wonders of the sea,
my husband, Greg*

ONE

I MOVED FROM LUBBOCK, TEXAS, TO HERMOSA BEACH, CALIFORNIA, EXACTLY EIGHT DAYS, FOUR *hours, and fifty-seven minutes before the beginning of my junior year. Eight days, four hours, and fifty-seven minutes to unpack my boots, hang up my Tim McGraw poster, and find a new friend, which was entirely my mother's idea. I had spent my whole lifetime in Lubbock working my way up the social food chain. When I left town, I was on the bottom of the B-list with only one true friend. What made my mom think I could find a new one in eight days, four hours, and thirty-six minutes before the start of classes? (Time passes when you're blogging.) The way I figured, I had barely enough time to decide what to wear.*

Molly rested her hands on the keyboard of her laptop and fixed her eyes on the unpacked boxes that rose from floor to ceiling in her double-wide trailer like cardboard mountains. She wanted to post that stark image on her

MySpace blog, but that meant actually finding her digital camera. Deciding it was worth the effort, she maneuvered through the cramped living room, scanning the hand-written box labels. She ripped open one marked MOLLY'S STUFF only to find a carton full of mismatched Tupperware containers. So much for her mom's stellar organizational skills. Once more, Molly puzzled over her mom's sudden decision to leave Texas for California. Lynette had packed up their sprawling, ranch-style home in a record thirty-six hours and fifty-two minutes, exactly two weeks before escrow closed. They left the Lone Star State under the cloak of darkness like thieves stealing away in the middle of the night. For miles and miles, Molly prayed that her mother would U-turn their Ryder truck around and head back to West Texas. She didn't give up hope until they pulled into Williams, Arizona. There, at the Gateway to the Grand Canyon, she finally accepted that life as she knew it had officially ended.

Molly had spent three days sorting through stacks of mislabeled boxes, unsuccessfully searching for her favorite pieces of clothing. She finally found her camera in a con-tainer marked KITCHEN SPICES. Squeezing her small frame in between the boxes, she held the camera at arm's length and started snapping. Her eyes were her best feature, mainly because she had long lashes, which meant she didn't have to wear mascara, a wonderful asset because she thought makeup in general was more trouble than it was worth. But the problem was that the angle she chose unintentionally made the boxes look *gi-normous* and made Molly appear even smaller than she was. Barely over five feet tall, Molly was petite, a term she hated. She felt that labeling people was degrading to begin with and that labeling them by size was a major crime. She was built straight up and down, with no real girly curves. She was slender enough, but she was soft. Exercise was not her forte, which was why she was very proud of her flat, washboard stomach. When commented upon, she liked to point out that she had never done a sit-up in her life.

Lynette had left an hour earlier for her late shift at a defense contractor plant just south of LAX. Molly was effectively on her own, which she didn't mind. Not one bit. Only a little hungry, even though it was almost six thirty, Molly wandered from the living room into the kitchen, which only took about one and a half seconds. Her West Texas home had three whole rooms in between the kitchen and living room. Molly felt strange about a new family moving into her old house, as if the walls held private memories and secrets that the new family had access to, instead of her. If walls could talk, would they whisper what terrible thing had happened in those rooms? As far as Molly knew, her parents

3

hardly even fought. What could have been so hideous that it would make her mother leave her dad, file papers for a divorce, and give up a beautiful suburban home for a double-wide in Hermosa? Every time she questioned her mom about the divorce or the move, Lynette offered up the same flimsy excuse: "Well, I don't want to say anything bad about your dad."

On the chipped Formica table was a pair of chopsticks, a box of microwave ramen noodles, a gerbera daisy plopped in an empty soda can, and a hand-scribbled note that read: "See you in the morning, honey. Enjoy your dinner." Back in Lubbock, her mom cooked a home-made dinner every single night. They only did take-out when she was sick. Was her mom's cheery note some kind of joke, a feeble stab at the ironic? Molly sighed, twisted her thick, shoulder-length, coffee-colored hair into a bun at the back of her neck, and grabbed one of the chopsticks off the table to secure it. She scooped up her house keys off the table and left through the back door.

Outside were thirty mobile homes crowded on a cracked asphalt pad. To the west an enormous sand dune, covered in verbena, towered over the park ominously. It seemed to Molly like one little tremor in the earth's shelf could send an avalanche of sand down upon them, bury the entire park, and condemn the residents to a gruesome death.

"Marineland Mobile Park has been here for sixty years and has survived several major quakes," the landlady, Miz Boyer, told them when they moved in, offended by Molly's doomsday scenario. None of the residents of Marineland Mobile Park knew their landlady's first name, so they all pronounced "Miz" with a "z" because that's the way she said it.

Molly walked under the iron archway, leaving the dreary trailer park behind. She stepped onto Pier Avenue, the busy main street of her new home, a tiny Southern California beach hamlet whose brightly painted storefronts were at odds with Molly's mood. She passed a bakery called Yak and Yeti's, a sushi bar that was actually a bar, a French lingerie store, and a funky British record store (and, yes, it actually said RECORD on the neon sign). She saw girls wearing bikinis and belly rings, old men in Hawaiian shirts walking their dogs, young singles in Juicy Couture smocked dresses, soccer moms corralling their charges, Emo rockers in too-tight, too-old clothes, kids on skateboards, and Hollywood hipsters down for the day. Most were wearing flip-flops—so many, in fact, that Molly wondered if the thong sandal was the California state shoe. In West Texas she had been on the cutting edge of cool, but the cultural sand had shifted. Here in this beach town, she felt like somebody's grandmother in her cowboy boots with yellow roses, a pair of Bermuda shorts, and a vintage tee from Willie Nelson's Fourth of July Picnic, circa 1984.

When a four-year-old girl in teeny, tiny flip-flops whispered to her mother as she pointed at Molly's cowboy boots, Molly ducked into a funky surf shop with "used boards— fifty bucks" lined up like dominoes outside the front.

Inside, she quickly moved past the racks of expensive, designer surf wear (Roxy, Quicksilver, and Hurley) to the back of the store, where an entire wall was devoted to ultra-cool flip-flops. The choices were endless: brown leather, black suede, thin or thick straps, tan with turquoise, and ones with beaded medallions. They even had hot pink studded with rhinestones, dressy enough to wear to the prom. All of them were overpriced, in Molly's opinion. In her former life, Molly thought nothing of paying fifty dollars for a pair of shoes and hundreds for cowboy boots, but forty dollars for a little leather strap attached between your toes seemed outrageous. Molly flagged down a young salesman with tattoo-covered arms.

"Do you have any plain, ol' rubber flip-flops?" Molly asked.

"Do we look like Wal-Mart?" he asked.

As if Wal-mart would hire a guy with spiked purple hair and shoulder-to-wrist tattoos.

"Do you have anything a little less expensive?" she asked.

He pointed dismissively to a sale bin of rubber thongs

adorned with garish plastic flowers, last year's model on sale for a mere five bucks. Partial to roses, as evidenced by the ones on her boots, she chose a pair adorned with pale yellow rosebuds and left the store with her boots tucked away in a Roxy shopping bag, feeling much better about her outfit, if not herself.

The palm-tree-lined piazza that led to the pier was jumping. It was last call for summer, and happy hour was cranked up to maximum speed. Twenty-something singles spilled out of the bars onto the patios, soaking up the warm sun along with their beers. Next door to the bar, Molly spotted a group of kids more her age at Java Boy, celebrating the last week of vacation with legal intoxicants, fancy coffee drinks. Molly was struck by how fused these kids seemed with their surroundings, how perfectly at home. She longed to be one of the girls sitting at the table under the awning, sipping a frothy cappuccino and flirting with the easy laugh of confidence. As Molly passed by, one of the guys at the table actually smiled at her. While Molly mentally scrambled for a clever icebreaker, she was clipped from behind, her feet jerked out from under her. She landed unceremoniously on her butt, right in front of the guy she was trying to impress. A blur shot passed her, what looked to be a dog leashed to a skateboard.

And, in fact, that's just what it was. Molly had been

tripped up by a local legend, a tall, tanned, thirty-year-old woman who used her pit bull to power her skateboard.

Everyone at the table started laughing. They couldn't help themselves. It was hard to tell who looked more ridiculous: Molly splayed out on the pavement, or the woman on the skateboard, screaming at her leashed dog to keep going. Molly wasn't about to be the victim of a hit-and-run by some weird California New Age version of a dogsled. She struggled to her feet and yelled, "Hey you—stop! Come back here."

The skateboarder yanked the leash, and the pit bull careened to a stop. She flipped off her skateboard and turned around, revealing enormous, surgically enhanced breasts. "Why?" she yelled back.

"Well, I might be hurt. Did you ever think about that?"

"Well, what do you expect me to do?" the woman asked snarkily, and the dog growled.

An unidentified male voice rang out, "How about you start with saying, 'I'm sorry'!"

Molly turned to see the owner of that amazing, compassionate voice. She involuntarily grabbed a small intake of air; it was almost a gasp. He looked as good as he sounded, the poster boy for California cool. He wore board shorts and a serious expression. His tan chest was as bare as his feet, and he had deep, soulful eyes. He scowled at the skateboarder, demanding justice. She flipped her hair haughtily.

"Asshole," the skateboarder replied, not about to be lectured on social protocol by someone ten years her junior, even if he was stunning. She jumped on her board, cracked the leash, and her pit bull took off at a run, presumably to terrorize other unsuspecting pedestrians. Before Molly could turn to thank him, the barefoot Adonis tucked his surfboard under his arm and disappeared into the surf shop. She brushed off her shorts and continued, as grateful for his show of kindness as she was disappointed in having lost the opportunity of meeting him face-to-face.

Molly reached the end of the plaza and gazed out across the expanse of white sand leading to the water. The young surfer's good looks and soulful stare may have made her gasp, but this view of the ocean took her breath away. To the north, the Santa Monica Mountains pushed their way far out to the sea, and to the south, the lush, green hills of Palos Verdes rose majestically. Stretched out in front of her was the boundless Pacific Ocean, a god-touched sunset spilling into the azure waters in pools of fiery color. As she gazed across the vista, she considered the fact that she now lived at the place where land ends.

CRASH! Molly's reverie was interrupted by the banging of trash cans. An old guy—at least thirty-five, maybe even forty—staggered out of a raggedy bar called the Paradise Inn and smashed into the trash cans lined up outside. He had a scraggly beard, a short ponytail, and skin aged by the sun to a leathery brown. He looked vaguely familiar; she thought she recognized him from Marineland Mobile Park, that he lived in the fourth trailer from the gate, the one with half a dozen surfboards parked out front. Clearly drunk, he fumbled for his keys.

"Are you okay?" Molly asked, walking toward him. Five minutes ago she had been victimized by a stranger only to be the recipient of the kindness from another one. She decided to pay forward the kindness by lending a helping hand to a fellow human being who could clearly use assistance. It was the right thing to do. And, besides, she needed all the karmic brownie points she could muster. "Look, you're too messed up to drive. Can I call somebody to come get you?" she asked, flipping out her cell.

He looked up at her, startled. A wave of gratitude passed over his face just before he turned pea green and blew chow. Molly jumped back, but not quickly enough. Her brand-new flip-flops, not to mention her feet, were sprayed by his vomit. Speechless, he waved apologetically and weaved his way back to the Paradise Inn, flinging open the door and disappearing back into the bowels of that raucous establishment. Stunned, Molly stared at her ruined sandals.

Back home, Molly returned to her blog.

Okay, let's recap. My new home is a double-wide in a tacky trailer park. I can't find the box with my clothes in it. And so far today, I've been knocked on my butt, laughed at, and thrown up on. Makes you wonder what could possibly happen next. Oh yeah, school. Perfect.

TWO

**MOLLY WALKED THROUGH THE CROWDED,
LOCKER-LINED CORRIDOR OF BEACH HIGH**
clutching a piece of paper with her locker combination scribbled on it. Her old school, Garfield High, had been named after an obscure president, which was infinitely better than the blandly generic "Beach." And her new school's mascot was even more embarrassing. Not a fierce cougar or an imposing bear or a chivalrous knight. No, they were the Waves, the *Beach Waves*. Molly wondered if Beach fans yelled "Tsunami!" at football games to intimidate rival teams.

The worst part of going to a new school was mapping out the territory: finding your locker, locating the clean bathrooms, and discovering which group owned which piece of lunchroom turf. The key to survival was figuring out the lay of the land as quickly as possible. Her first year at Garfield, she banded together with four other freshmen who had known one another in middle school and were united by their common fear of upperclassmen. This time and at this school, she had to go it alone.

Molly's locker was located at the end of the hall on the bottom of a stack of three. Blocking it was the senior beauty queen, Jenn, who was holding court with her ladies-in-waiting, all of whom wore dresses over jeans, one of those popular yet terrible clothing trends that Molly found super annoying.

"Excuse me," Molly said politely as she edged past her, "I need to get to my locker."

As Molly bent over to unlock her combination, she unintentionally brushed against Jenn's chest with her elbow.

"You touched me," Jenn said, offended.

"I'm sorry, but if you could move a little to the left, then I could actually open my locker," Molly said.

Jenn held her ground and continued relating the boring details of a shopping expedition into Beverly Hills. Molly had to contort like a pretzel in order to stuff her books in her locker. When she straightened, she accidentally grazed the hip pocket of Jenn's three-hundred-dollar jeans.

"You touched me again," Jenn said, this time outraged. She raised her voice so that absolutely everyone in the crowded hallway could hear, "What a lesbian!"

Everyone turned and stared at poor Molly, the girl who hated labels and who suddenly through no fault of her own had one. She made a hasty retreat, followed by stares and whispers, and ducked into her first-period English class, which was thankfully uneventful.

Second period, Molly entered the band hall tentatively. She slipped into a seat in the third row, not too far and not too close to the front, a little off to the side, sitting next to a very officious-looking girl wearing Oliver Peoples. She tossed Molly a casual nod and a half smile, "You must be the new girl."

Wow, word traveled fast.

"The Texas lesbian," the girl added.

Too fast. Way too fast.

Molly cleared her throat. "I'm Molly Browne—that's Brown with an 'e,' and, personally, I don't have anything against lesbians. My lab partner in Lubbock was one."

"Neither do I," she said interrupting. "I'm Andrea Longley, first chair clarinet and vice president of the junior class."

Molly thought it odd if not pretentious for Andrea to introduce herself as the vice president of anything, but she was so grateful for the chance at conversation, she decided to let it pass. "So where do you live?" Andrea continued.

"Pretty close to the school," Molly said, hedging, not wanting to reveal any embarrassing geographical details.

"Everybody lives close to the school. You can walk from one end of town to the other in twenty minutes. Are you east or west of Sepulveda?" Andrea asked, referencing the six-lane thoroughfare that separated the beach cities with a string of interminably long traffic lights.

"West," Molly answered truthfully.

"Excellent," Andrea commented. In Southern California, west was always more desirable because it was closer to the beaches. "Are you in the sand section?"

"Kinda. I mean, there's a lot of sand near our house. An entire sand dune, as a matter of fact," Molly said.

"What street are you on?"

"Marineland Park Drive," Molly said.

"The trailer park? I thought only surf bums and really old people lived there."

From Andrea's expression, Molly knew intuitively that she had lost major social ground. She scrambled to make it up. "Well, it's only temporary. We're building a house on the Strand." Which was LIE NUMBER ONE.

"I live on the Strand. Which one is yours?"

The Strand was a twelve-foot walkway that separated the multimillion-dollar mansions on beachfront property from the sand. Molly struggled to remember the cross streets of the new homes under construction she had noticed on her outings last week.

"The one near Eighth," she ventured.

"Oh, the Cape Cod," Andrea confirmed Molly's best guess. "Cool. We'll be neighbors. Let me see your schedule," Andrea said, grabbing it from Molly, who breathed a sigh of relief. "What are you doing in sixth-period PE?" she asked accusingly.

"My band credits from Texas didn't transfer as PE credit."

"So do a sport."

"I'm not really that athletic."

"Everybody at Beach has got something. Even the nerdiest nerds run cross-country. I've lettered in three varsity sports already—lacrosse, tennis, and pole vaulting. And, just so you know, there's a reason they call sixth-period physical education 'Loser PE,'" she warned.

The bell rang, and their band instructor lumbered in, carrying three extra music stands and an armload of sheet music. Stealing in unnoticed behind him was the young surfer she had seen the day before. Molly couldn't believe it; he was all that and musical, too. Andrea nudged Molly. "Is he hot or what?"

In guarded whispers as he walked toward them, Andrea explained that Kai's Hawaiian mother had named her son

Kai, which meant "the sea" in Hawaiian. A legend at Beach, he grew up in the reefs off Kauai and came of age in the kelp beds off Catalina. True to his name, he was a bona fide waterman and some said he was more comfortable swimming in the ocean than he was walking on land.

Molly almost died when he slid into the empty seat next to her. She couldn't help but notice that his hair was still wet. He shook it off his face; she caught a whiff of salt, as if he had just emerged from the ocean instead of the shower. "Hi," she said softly.

"Hi," he said back, flashing a million-dollar smile. He wasn't flirting with her; he just had a great smile.

While the gangly band director, Mr. Fauver, organized his desk and role book, the room buzzed with dozens of conversations. Molly took advantage of the opportunity to start one of her own. "Listen, thanks for yesterday."

Kai looked confused. "I'm sorry. Do I know you?"

Molly turned away, embarrassed. She thought she had made a good impression, only to discover she had made no impression at all. She was invisible.

And invisible she felt through the next two classes. No one else besides Jenn was intentionally mean to her. No, this was worse. No one was anything to her. She was completely and totally ignored. In third period, she actually text-messaged herself so that in fourth she could pretend to

17

be connected. When the bell for lunch rang, she slinked her way through one of the few locker-lined inside hallways. Beach High, like so many California schools, took advantage of the temperate weather. The school was divided into a series of smaller buildings, blocks of rooms opening directly to outside spaces and connected by foliage-lined pathways. Molly was relieved when she spotted Andrea strolling across the manicured grounds toward the main courtyard. Because Andrea had been borderline nice to her earlier that day, Molly ran to catch up with her and asked her where the lunchroom was.

"The what?"

"The lunchroom. Well, that's what we called in Texas. You know, the cafeteria."

"We don't have one. We eat outside in the courtyard."

"What do you do when it rains?"

"It never rains in Southern California," she said flippantly.

Molly had watched television coverage of huge hills of mud collapsing onto houses in Malibu, and she knew damn well where mud came from; it came from rain. But she wasn't about to pick an argument with her only semisolid connection in this impenetrable school.

They turned into the crowded Quadrangle, where the students had divided into smaller groups who claimed the territory on the first day of the fall semester that would be their lunchtime turf for the rest of the year. Andrea always sat with other girls in ASB, which stood for Associated Student Body, the rah-rah planners of Winter Formals and hurricane relief fund-raisers. She was the vice president of that group as well.

"Hey, do you mind if I eat lunch with you?"

"Sorry," she said, gesturing to the girls who were waving her over, "but there's not really room."

Painfully alone, Molly considered her options. Having none, she ducked down the open-air corridor leading to the band room. The door was ajar, so she stepped inside, looking for asylum. Sitting on the back row was a pimply faced, overweight freshman tuba player who ripped open the second of his third bag of Ding Dongs. Molly sat down in a chair in the front row in the far corner, an entire room away from her fellow outcast. And, together, yet apart, they ate their lunch in silence.

Molly could not wait for the day to be over. Her last class was physical education. In the locker room she changed into baggy, school-issued gym shorts and an oversize tee with an ocean wave plastered across the front that overwhelmed her small frame. She entered the gymnasium, scanned the faces of classmates, and knew immediately why it was called Loser PE. It was a room full of misfits, the dregs of high school humanity, some in defiance of the social order and some victims of it, but each and every one was a certified outsider. Molly had nothing against outsiders, any more than she had anything against lesbians. It was just that she didn't want to be the former and she hadn't been born the latter. Sadly, the only one face in the crowd she recognized was her lunch buddy, the Ding Dong tuba player. And when he saw her, he screamed, "Are you following me?"

This was beyond bad. Destined to be the number one loser among a gym full of them, she turned and fled before role was even called.

Molly marched past the attendance ladies, argued her way past the gatekeeper secretary at the next desk, and barged into her counselor's office. Ms. Rawlings was an overworked, underpaid, extremely tired lady in her mid fifties, who had over four hundred charges in her care and on any given Monday, half of them were unhappy.

"Is there any way I can get out of taking PE?"

Ms. Rawlings sighed. "I told you, Molly. Only marching band counts as physical education credit. Jazz band is not considered an aerobic activity."

"Have you ever seen a hundred-pound girl play the sax? Talk about aerobic," Molly insisted.

Ms. Rawlings smiled. There was something about this

girl she liked, although she wasn't completely clear what is was. "Why don't you sign up for marching band?"

"I can't walk and chew gum at the same time, much less march and play."

"Okay. You could try out for a sport," she suggested.

"Not a good idea," Molly said.

"Then I'm sorry, Molly. You'll have to take PE."

"This is so unfair. If I stay in sixth-period PE, I will die and I'm not exaggerating," Molly said, melting into her chair like the Wicked Witch of the West.

"Maybe you should consider drama," Ms. Rawlings said, deadpan. "You seem to have a talent for it."

"Will it count as PE?" she asked, and on Ms. Rawlings's look of frustration, she added quickly, "Okay, I'll do a sport, but do you have one that doesn't involve a ball?"

"What about track and field?"

"I'm not very good at running and I don't like to jump over things."

"Molly, there are five other kids with scheduling issues waiting for me. Can you try to be a little more cooperative?"

"Okay, how about something in the field of aquatics?" Molly asked. She had spent most of the Texas summer in a swimming pool to escape the sweltering heat.

"Well, we have a swim team, a diving team, a water polo team . . ."

"Water polo involves a ball," Molly pointed out.

"Right," Ms. Rawlings noted. "What about water ballet?"

Concocting a weird vision of pink tutus floating in an over-chlorinated pool, Molly dismissed that idea and looked through the course catalog herself. She stopped at the next-to-last entry. "What's this?" she asked, pointing to big bold letters that read **SURF ED**.

Ms. Rawlings explained that kids could, in fact, surf away their PE requirement. The class met two mornings a week at six o'clock on the beach, and students didn't have to come to school until second period every day. Molly was not a morning person, but the idea of sleeping late three times a week trumped having to get up early twice. Besides, how cool was it to get class credit for hanging out at the beach. She grabbed the drop/add slip and began filling it out enthusiastically.

"Molly, do you even know how to surf?" Ms. Rawlings wondered.

"Why do you ask?"

"Because knowing how to surf and being ocean-aware is a prerequisite for taking this class."

"No, I meant why would you assume that I don't know how to surf?"

"West Texas is a little far from the ocean."

"My family summered at Padre Island," Molly said, which was LIE NUMBER TWO. She had never even seen the Gulf of Mexico.

LIE NUMBER THREE wasn't exactly a lie. When Molly got home from school, she told her mother she needed fifty dollars for "school supplies." She took her mother's hard-earned cash and returned to the surf shop, where she sorted through the stack of fifty-buck long boards. She found one that spoke to her. It was a nine-foot, seven-inch standout, the longest board in the rack. If there was one thing every well-brought-up Texas girl knew, it was that when it came to diamonds, hair, and cars, size actually did matter and "bigger meant better." Molly speculated that the same might hold true for surfboards. The surly salesman who had sold her the flip-flops watched slack-jawed as she pulled it off the rack and tried to maneuver it to the counter to pay for it. "Are you sure a little girl like you can manage that monster?"

Molly exploded. "Do you think that just because I have a Texas accent and I'm not a big, strapping California blonde that I can't handle myself in the water?"

"I just think you'd be happier with a seven-footer," he said, gesturing to a rack of brand-new boards, which started at five hundred dollars. Molly was not about to be conned into buying a board she couldn't afford by a not-so-smooth-talking salesman with a pierced tongue and tattooed arms. So she bought the used one against his advice and when she got home, she tucked it in the side yard, out of view.

While Molly had been shopping, her mother had been unpacking. The contents of half a dozen boxes filled every available tabletop in the living room. Lynette was hunkered over Molly's laptop.

"Do you need some help putting this stuff away?" Molly asked her mom, puzzled.

"Actually, I'm taking inventory. I decided to sell some of the stuff we don't really need," she said as she created a false feedback report on her new eBay account to establish her credibility.

Molly looked at the items on the table, relics from her old life. She picked up a chipped dinner plate and touched the soft pink roses that circled the rim with a sudden surge of longing. "You're not going to sell these dishes, are you?"

"Sweetie, we have four sets of dishes and the shelf space for one," her mom explained.

"We had plenty of shelf space in the old house," Molly snapped, and slammed the door to her bedroom, the tension between mother and daughter settling on the room like dust.

That evening while her mother worked late into the night moonlighting on eBay, Molly went to bed early. She programmed her iPod to go off at five thirty. Afraid of over-sleeping, she wore her bikini and board shorts to bed so that she wouldn't have to waste precious time in the morning getting dressed. She snuggled under her quilt and waited for sleep that didn't come until three hours before it was time to get up.

THREE

JUST GETTING TO THE BEACH WAS AN ORDEAL. MOLLY'S NEW BOARD WAS NOT ONLY long, it was heavy. After two blocks she was convinced that it weighed as much as she did. She parked it outside Java Boy, secretly hoping someone would steal it. She bought a triple-shot latte and checked her watch. Thankfully, she was ahead of schedule. She arrived at the beach ten minutes early, assuming she would be the first one there. But she was wrong. A dozen kids, the Dawn Patrol, were already on the sand, waxing their boards and putting on their wet suits. AJ—tall, lanky, and topped with a mop of uncontrollable curls—opened his extra-large sports bag as Molly approached. AJ was known as the accessory man; he owned every piece of surf gear imaginable—rash guard, booties, helmet, gloves, and six different wet suits.

"You the new grommet?" he asked Molly.

"I guess so," Molly said, having no idea that a *grommet*

referred to a young surfer. "I'm Molly Browne, and that's Brown with an 'e,'" she said, holding out her hand, trying a little too hard.

"As in unsinkable?" AJ asked, proud of himself for being so clever.

"Just so you know, I've heard that one before," Molly said.

His buddy, Buzz, scanned the horizon. "Waves are for shit today. Nothing but two-foot mushburgers," he said, spitting for emphasis. Buzz, whose nickname was derived from short-cropped hair, currently tipped bright red, looked at Molly through his wraparound glasses. Buzz always wore his shades, even in the fog.

"They look more like four feet to me," Molly said. She had no idea that waves were measured from their back, so that a two-footer did appear like four feet at its face. The guys looked at her oddly. Intuitively knowing she had made an error of some kind, she let the wet sand below the tide-line squish between her toes.

The smallest of the group, Flea, noticed her nervousness. He was barely bigger than Molly, a wiry little guy whose small build was an asset on the takeoff. "Are you okay? You look a little pale."

"I need more coffee," Molly said as she took another sip. "God, I hate early morning."

"And sometimes I think the sunrise is so good, why even bother with the rest of the day," a distinctive voice rang out from behind her.

She turned and saw that the owner of that familiar voice was Kai, who sauntered up, already wet and casually carrying his board under his arm. "Swells' breaking nice on the north side of the pier."

"You've already been in the water?" Molly asked incredulously.

"Yeah, I got here at five," he said.

"You really are a morning person," Molly said, making small talk.

"Absolutely," he said. "What about you?"

"Night owl, definitely," she responded.

"Then what are you doing here?"

"Getting credit, same as you," Molly said a little too defensively.

"No," he said evenly. "I'm here because there's no other place I'd rather be."

She hated the self-righteous ring to his voice. She knew then that her California poster boy was nothing more than an obnoxious surfer dude: too cool, too confident and, worst of all, too much of a morning person.

"Where's Waldo?" Kai asked his crew.

"I don't know, but there's his board," Flea said,

pointing to a Rincon Stinger leaning against the deserted lifeguard hut.

"That dude's always MIA," Kai said.

"Is Waldo our instructor?" Molly asked.

"Instructor? That's a good one," Buzz said, laughing.

"Duke's the man in charge," Flea added. "Sometimes he's a little late, but he always shows. Problem is, we can't officially go into the water till he gets here—right, Kai?" he said pointedly.

Molly was not surprised to learn that Kai was also too cool for rules.

A few minutes later, Waldo, a totally tan, surf-toned boy, emerged from the empty lifeguard hut with Riki, the only other girl besides Molly on the beach so far. Waldo was the latest on Riki's long list of conquests; she had been hooking up with seniors since eighth grade. You could tell by the smug look on their faces that they'd been indulging in what Waldo referred to with a chuckle and a nudge as "the breakfast of champions." Molly wondered how anyone could even think about sex so early in the a.m., much less have some.

"Sup, brah," Waldo said as he greeted Kai with slaps and complicated hand signals that rivaled any Westside gang. Riki hung back, adjusting her bikini bra strap before stepping into her wet suit. Noticing Molly for the first time, Waldo looked her over from top to bottom. "Cool board."

"It's vintage," Molly said.

"So where's your wet suit, grommet?" he asked.

Molly noted that the entire Dawn Patrol was sporting neoprene, wet suits made of air-injected rubber. She was the only one without one. "Most of my stuff is still in boxes. I haven't finished unpacking," she said.

"I thought I recognized you. You're the new girl from Texas, right?" he added matter-of-factly. "The lesbian."

"I am from Texas, but I'm NOT a lesbian," she said, trying to set the record straight.

"Good to know," Waldo said as he began waxing his board. Overhearing, Riki slipped up from behind and slapped him on the back.

"Are we the only girls in the class?" Molly asked her.

"Duh?" Riki gestured to the beach full of boys. "Could it be more apparent?"

"Surf Ed.'s not really a girl thing," Buzz said.

"Oh, come on. Didn't any of y'all see *Blue Crush*? Girl surfers rule," Molly said.

"Not at this break," Buzz replied.

Riki explained, "Look, there are six of us divas on the Surf Team, which trains in the afternoon, but no one besides me has the patience to put up with their 'tude this early in the morning," she said, pointing at the five major players of the Dawn Patrol.

"Divas? Y'all sing as well as surf?" Molly asked.

The group eyed her suspiciously. Even a grommet knew that *diva* was surf lingo for girl surfer.

"Where did you say you learned to surf?" Kai asked.

"Gulf of Mexico," Molly said, unblinking.

Riki zeroed in on Molly's bikini, which bagged from age, the spandex having lost its stretch. "I've never surfed the Gulf, but the bikini you're wearing could prove to be a problem in our waters. One wipeout and you'll be topless," Riki warned.

"Hey, we got no problem with that," Waldo said, followed by hoots and hollers from his compadres.

"The Big Kahuna has arrived," Flea said, pointing to an approaching figure striding across the beach. The man's face was not readily discernible because of the glare of the rising sun. At about a hundred feet away, Duke Updike, a forty-four-year-old surfing legend, powerfully built with ravaged good looks, stopped to give the thumbs-up signal. The kids on the shoreline zipped up their wet suits, grabbed their boards, and headed for the water like lemmings.

Only Molly remained, staring with disbelief as the man got closer. She realized for the first time just how small this small town was. Duke was none other that the guy she had seen two days before exiting the sleazy bar, the same guy who had thrown up on her flip-flops. If he recognized her, he didn't give any indication, and she wasn't about to bring up his drunken and semi-disorderly conduct because it didn't seem respectful on her first day in his surfing class. Besides, he was clean-shaven now and seemed perfectly sober. She waited patiently for him to introduce himself or to ask for a course-add slip from her counselor. But he didn't say a word. He zeroed in on her with an intense stare that lay somewhere in between the gaze of a Zen master and the look her first dog gave her when he was confused.

"Been a while since I've seen a pint-size girl on a Malibu board," Duke said, commenting on her ten-footer. He sat down on the sand, and his gaze shifted from her to the sea. Together he and Molly watched the surfers paddle out beyond the breakers, sit on their boards, and let their feet dangle in the water, rolling with the swells and casually talking to one another as they waited to catch the first wave. A well-formed two-footer came along, and Flea was the first to take off demonstrating how he had earned his nickname. Molly assumed it referenced his size, but actually it had to do with the way he popped up on his feet like a flea jumping off a dog. He launched his board off the lip of the wave, free-falling down the face with the breaking white water. He made it look easy. Nearing the shore, he kicked out at the last minute, pulled in his board by the leash, and yelled back at her, "Surf's up. What are you waiting for, Molls?"

"Inspiration," she yelled back.

Scooping up a handful of sand and letting it sift through his fingers, Duke smiled. If he was worried about the new girl, he didn't show it. He was curious to see how she handled herself. The mushy waves were softer, more forgiving. He figured she'd be okay.

She walked to the water with a simple plan. A quick study, she believed if she watched the guys surfing long enough, she could figure out how to do it. Learn by example—that was her theory. But first, she had to get herself and her board through, over or under the breakers and out to the calm spot. Holding her board over her head—she couldn't manage it under one arm like the others—she stepped her first foot into the Pacific Ocean.

The water was frigid. No wonder the other kids wore wet suits. The beginning of school in Lubbock was always hotter than hell. She tried to summon the memory of that dry, unbearable heat and imagine how good this icy water would feel under more West Texas circumstances. She was only ankle deep when the first rush of white water hit her. The surge from the undertow was so powerful, it almost knocked her over; she had to struggle to regain her footing.

She waited for a lull between the sets before making her initial charge. In between waves, she launched her board and climbed on belly-down. Even though she paddled like hell, she made no forward progress. She hit the wave on the lip, the most powerful part. Just before impact, she grabbed the rails of her surfboard and tired to push the nose under the turbulence. Experienced surfers knew to head directly into the wave, but Molly got turned sideways. The white water knocked her off her board, and she crashed into the brink. She came up sputtering and spewing; her board was flopping around uncontrollably, a ten-foot hazard in the water. She panicked when she looked up and saw Kai surfing toward her on a collision course.

"Get out of the way," she yelled, when a second wave knocked her over.

In over to avoid running directly over the struggling surfer, Kai was forced to kick out of his mighty fine ride and assume the turtle position. He rolled his board, held on underneath, and frog-kicked his way clear of her. After the wave passed, he rolled his board back over. He was furious; every grommet knew that the surfer up and riding had right of way over the one paddling out.

Molly popped up a few feet away, coughing and holding on to her board like it was a life preserver.

"Hey, newbie, don't you know the rules of the road?" he screamed.

"Yeah, stay alive!" she screamed back, swallowing even more seawater.

"You need help?" he asked, softening.

And even though she did, she wasn't about to ask him for it. "No thanks, I can manage."

He shrugged and paddled through the break like it was nothing. On the beach, Duke moved farther down the sand to keep a closer eye on the new girl who was clearly having trouble. Duke never offered suggestions or advice unless the kids asked for it. Still, nobody had ever drowned in Surf Ed. Not on his watch. And he wasn't about to let Molly be the first.

For the next hour, Molly waged a brave and valiant war against the mushburger waves. Although she made countless attempts, she couldn't get past knee-deep water. Worn out and feeling like a piece of driftwood tempest-tossed, she was ready to throw in the towel. Not only could she not surf, she couldn't even past get past the breakers. Luckily, Duke whistled from the shore and waved them in, signaling class was over.

Soaked and bedraggled, Molly trudged through the billowing foam, shaking the water out of her hair, shivering from the cold and dragging her long board behind her. It whipped against the sand in the wash. A flock of gulls swept past her, and their mocking caws sounded like laughter. Duke waited for her above the waterline. He shook his head sadly as she approached. By his look, she knew that he knew that she was a fraud.

"You don't know how to surf, do you?" he asked.

For a split second she considered making up yet another lie. But when he lowered his chin and looked her straight in the eye, she thought better of it. "No, this is my first time," Molly said.

Flea, Buzz, Waldo, and Kai came in out of the water and packed up their gear nearby so they could listen in on the conversation. Molly felt their indignant stares.

"Did they tell you that you had to know how to surf to be in this class?" Duke asked.

"Yes," Molly said, waiting for the inevitable. When he said nothing, she asked, "Are you gonna kick me out?"

Duke shaded his forehead with his hand and looked out to sea, where he spotted the sleek, silver body of a dolphin visible within a curling arc of water. As the dolphin surfed down the face of the wave and disappeared under the breaker, Duke turned to Molly. "You need a shorter board."

"Excuse me?" Molly said.

"You need a wide, steady board that's only a couple feet taller than you. The board you got is too squirrelly, too hard to paddle, and not buoyant enough for a beginner."

"It was the only board I could afford," Molly said.

"I didn't say you had to buy a new board. I just said you'll never learn to surf on that one." Duke turned to leave. "See you Thursday."

Molly was speechless, a rare occurrence.

"Saved by the dolphin," Waldo said, explaining that a dolphin sighting brought good luck all day long.

And sending a little more luck her way, he pulled a jar of Vaseline from his surf bag and tossed it to her.

"What's this for?" she asked suspiciously.

"If you want to say warm in the water, here's what you do. Get to the beach early Thursday and rub this all over your body. And don't worry. I'll help you with the hard-to-reach spots," he said, leaning in closer to her.

Molly found his low, sexy voice annoying. She could tell that Waldo was the kind of guy who lived under the false assumption that all girls thrilled to his touch. "What is your real name?" she asked.

"Why?"

"Because I find your gift hugely offensive, and when I say, 'You're an asshole, Waldo,' I'd prefer to use the name your momma gave you," she said, pointing an accusing finger at the flummoxed Waldo. "Look, I don't want you touching me or coming on to me, and I have no intention of greasing up and becoming one of your surfette sex toys."

"I wasn't coming on to you," he said, his turn to be offended.

"You weren't?" she answered, backing down a little.

"Surprisingly, I'm unaware of its sexual uses, but a thin

layer of Vaseline really does keep you warm in the water."

"Good to know," she said, echoing his refrain.

"I just thought you could a little help until you find your wet suit," Waldo said.

"Thanks. And I'm sorry," Molly added.

"If she has a wet suit," Kai said, who, unlike Duke or Waldo, judged her severely. "So what else have you lied about?" he asked.

"Nothing," Molly said, lowering her eyes. And that was LIE NUMBER FOUR.

That morning in jazz band, Molly was the one to arrive with wet hair and the smell of salt still clinging to her skin. The rumor mill continued its grind, this time with something more akin to the truth. The little girl from Texas was taking on the early morning risers in Surf Ed. It may have been her imagination, but she thought that her fellow band members, especially Andrea, looked at her with new interest. One of the snare drummers said hello, and when jazz band was over, the second chair trombone walked with her to third period.

Home from school, Molly found a surprise waiting for her by the latticed stairs that led to her front door. It was a surfboard, this one about three feet shorter than the one she had bought and painted in faded psychedelic colors.

Although it was encrusted with wax and was dinged up nose to tail, Molly thought it was the most beautiful board she had ever seen. Taped to it was a note from Duke that read, "Sorry about ruining your flip-flops. I wanted to make it up to you and I thought a used board might be more useful than new *slippas*."

So he had known who she was. As grateful as she was for the new, used surfboard, she couldn't help but wonder why he'd given it to her. Was it because he believed in second chances? Or was it because he felt guilty? Or was he trying to buy her silence? She wouldn't learn the real reason until almost two months later.

FOUR

ON WEDNESDAY, MOLLY SLEPT IN, EXCUSED
FROM HER FIRST PERIOD CLASS BECAUSE OF
her Tuesday/Thursday Surf Ed. commitment, a perk she had
been looking forward to since she first signed up. According
to Molly, the world was divided into two types of people:
morning people and night people. She found it far more tol-
erable to be the latter, preferring night owls to early birds.
And she hated the way that naturally early risers—like Kai—
were always so critical of their more nocturnal brethren,
as if just waking up early made them morally superior to
people like Molly. And in her humble opinion, morning
people weren't morally superior; they were just driven, running from one place to another. That's why early risers often
did run someplace, like to the track or the gym.

If left to her own devices, Molly could sleep soundly
until mid-afternoon. Molly was so dead to the world on
Wednesday morning that she might have missed the third

day of school altogether had it not been for two greedy seagulls outside her trailer window, fighting over the remains of a sub sandwich. But it wasn't their warring shrieks that woke her up from her candy sweet dream; it was the screeching landlady who waged her own battle against the intrusion of the unruly, feathered offenders.

"Get out of here, you, hooligans," she hissed as she swung a long-handled broom in the birds' direction. The gulls' haughty reply was a flurry of flapping wings. They ignored her warnings and continued their midair battle over the rancid lunch meat.

"Hey, Miz Boyer," Duke shouted as he waxed his surfboard outside the front of his trailer. Several years back, when he first moved in, Duke casually asked his new landlady if "Miz" referred to *Mrs.* or *Ms.* or if it was a mispronunciation of *Miss.*

"My marital status is none of your damn business," Miz Boyer snapped. And for weeks afterward, every time he lugged his garbage cans to the street, she glowered at him with the same intense and unsettling look of disapproval she was now giving the birds. He felt their pain.

"Give the birds a break, Miz Boyer. They gotta eat too."

"Those aren't birds. Those are rats with wings!' she screamed back. And on precisely that note, Molly woke up.

She miraculously made it to school in fourteen minutes

flat, slipping into her second-period jazz band seconds before the tardy bell rang. To say she was a bit thrown together was putting it mildly. Her hair looked like it was a casualty of the seagull sandwich war of the morning. Her clothes looked like she had slept in them. And in fact, she had slept in the T-shirt. It was one of her favorites, a collector's item from Waylon Jennings's 1994 concert tour, old, worn, and soft as a baby's blanket. Rushing across the room, she tripped over the long legs of the snare drummer, the one who had actually said hello to her the day before and landed in the lap of the Ding Dong–eating tuba player, who commented loudly, "You can't get enough of me, can you?"

"I may have just reached my limit," Molly said as she straightened and scanned the room for an empty seat. Andrea waved her over to the vacant chair next to her, and she gratefully unloaded her thirty-pound backpack and hooked it to the back of her chair, which in turn collapsed, creating another ripple of laughter. Molly righted the chair, put the backpack on the floor beside it, and quickly sat down, hoping to fade into oblivion.

"You are drowning here," Andrea told Molly, who silently agreed. "But no worries. Because I'm going to help. You are my new special project."

Molly had never been anyone's project before, special or not, and while she couldn't help but wonder why one of

Beach High's stellar elite was willing to take her on, who was she to argue? Although Molly had never been partial to type-A personalities or to girls who managed to leak their list of accomplishments into the most casual of conversations, she recognized a social lifeline when she saw one. Besides, Andrea was right in her assessment. Molly was drowning, metaphorically and figuratively, in every sense of the word. So to be rescued by a totally irritating, self-absorbed, self-righteous do-gooder (And weren't all rescuers a little self-righteous and self-absorbed?) was better than drowning in anonymity.

"Why don't you come to my house after school? Around four, I think." Andrea pulled out her Blackberry to confirm. "No, make it four fifteen. I can fit you in between my lacrosse practice and physics tutor. Wait a minute. Make it four twenty, to be safe."

"Should I bring anything?" Molly asked.

"A new outfit," Andrea said, assessing Molly's shirt with a disapproving shudder.

"Do you know how hard it is to come by one of these?" Molly asked, not only attached to but proud of her Waylon T-shirt.

"I can only hope it's very, very difficult," Andrea said. "No one listens to country and western, much less wears it."

Molly pressed, defending a musical legend she herself

had never seen in concert. "I thought it was kinda cool to wear vintage concert tees."

"If it's the Rolling Stones, Aerosmith, Mötley Crüe—Metallica, even. Look, Molly, it's fine to be idiosyncratic and superfine to have eclectic taste. But country music is just plain weird."

"Does this mean I have to roll up my Tim McGraw poster and put it away?"

"Do you want my help or not?" Andrea asked.

"Yes, I do, and thank you. And I promise to pack away my boots and Western fringe jackets and listen to everything you have to say as long as you promise me that I don't have to start wearing dresses over my jeans," Molly said before she noticed that the lacy black top Andrea was wearing over her Frankie B.'s was in fact a 1960s version of the little black cocktail dress.

"Just kidding about that dress-over-the-jeans thing," Molly added, hoping Andrea wouldn't take further offense. But lucky for Molly, Andrea, who was texting on her Sidekick, never took the time to take offense when she was in the middle of a project.

Molly arrived at Andrea's house afternoon at precisely four thirty, and Andrea's mother, Terri Longley, answered the door. A California bleached blonde, she was an avid tennis player who often wore her tennis togs all day long. Today she wore her pale peach tennis skirt from her country club team, which showed off her well-shaped and tanned legs to perfection. She answered the door sipping from a glass of white wine, even though it was obviously too late for lunch and too early for before-dinner cocktails. Molly's own mother drank occasionally and only on the weekends. Molly considered her mother to be a social drinker and not a very sophisticated one. Lynette preferred her wine blushed and complained to Molly that there was not a pink Chablis to be had in Hermosa Beach; everybody in California drank red or white, Chardonnay or Merlot. In Molly's opinion, drinking wine alone on Tuesday at half past four in the afternoon could not be considered social drinking. It was just drinking—period. But not wanting to make judgments, Molly politely introduced herself to Andrea's mother, who insisted that she call her Terri.

"Is Andrea home yet? I was supposed to meet her after her lacrosse practice. We have a project we're fixin' to work on."

"Are you from Texas, Molly?"

"How did you know? Did my accent give it away?"

"No, my dear, it was your diction," Terri said with a soft smile. "Only someone from Texas would say 'supposed to' or 'fixin' to.' But now that you live here, you must try to correct your bad habits so you don't sound like a hick."

Terri invited her to wait, and Molly spent forty-five unbearable minutes "sharing" with Andrea's mother. There was a hint of desperation about Terri, like she was so lonely for company that she would actually relish a prolonged conversation with a sixteen-year-old who, by her own admission, had a diction problem. Molly had adult friends; age was not the problem. But Molly felt way too insecure to align herself with someone who seemed even more desperate than she was.

Andrea arrived home—finally—but with only seven minutes to spare for Molly before her physics tutor arrived. And she spent the entire seven minutes apologizing for being late and promising to set up another more convenient date as soon as possible. After all, she reassured her, Molly was her special project.

After being shuttled out of Andrea's beachfront mansion, Molly walked home, pausing at the top of the hill by the trailer park entrance. She turned toward the west and was almost blinded by the view of shimmery water in the strong afternoon sun. She knew, mainly because her mother reminded her every night since they had arrived, that everybody else in the world wanted to live in sunny Southern California. And she wondered what was wrong with her, why she felt drawn to the desolation of the Panhandle when she had Paradise in front of her.

The first thing she did when she got home was to call her best friend from Texas, but Katie's cell had been disconnected. Longing to touch some part of her past, to reconnect with the familiar, she dialed her old phone number. She still thought of it as *her* number even though it wasn't even connected to her old house anymore. The old number had traveled to the new condo her father bought, sight unseen. In fact, the phone number was one of the few trappings from his old life and their old house that he had taken with him. He didn't fight her mother for any of their shared belongings, which Molly thought that was very generous of him, especially considering her mom's dramatic and abrupt departure.

She listened to the ringing phone, oddly comforted by the connection to her former before-California life.

"Hello," a woman's voice answered. She had a light accent, Scandinavian maybe.

Startled, Molly hung up, wondering how she could have misdialed a number so permanently etched on her heart.

And then it occurred to her. Maybe she hadn't misdialed. What if her father had a girlfriend? The possibility of his seeking out other female friendships had been inevitable from the moment her mother backed out of the driveway and left him on his own. Everyone knew that Molly's dad couldn't manage more than one and half football games on a Saturday afternoon by himself. Midway through the second game, he'd get lonely and cajole her mom into dropping whatever weekend project she was working on to keep him company. And although Lynette often complained that her married life was a series of unfinished projects, Molly could tell that her mother was secretly pleased by the attention, by being wanted.

And now maybe her father wanted someone else. Angry at having been denied a comfortable ritual that connected her to the past, Molly flipped open her cell to see if she had misdialed. At the last minute she changed her mind; perhaps it would be better not to know for sure. So instead of checking her phone log, she put her old home number on speed dial so she wouldn't have to dial the numbers one by one again. Because that seemed just too painful.

On the Thursday session of Surf Ed., Molly was flabbergasted when AJ offered to loan her a wet suit he had outgrown. From his well-organized surf bag he pulled out a coal black neoprene shortie with a cobalt blue colored insert that ran across the shoulder and down the short sleeves and handed it to her. "This and the booties are all that's left from my blue period."

Grateful, Molly stepped into the suit, pulling the stretchy, synthetic rubber material over her legs and squeezing it over her bottom. Yesterday she had gone through her own "blue period" after the phone call to her father. But this morning, she woke up excited about the possibility of christening her new board in the water.

Molly zipped the suit up the front and adjusted the shoulders. It was nice and snug across the chest. "Thanks, AJ. It fits really well," she said, feeling more self-assured. The combination of a new board and a new outfit buoyed her confidence. She hoped that if she dressed the part, getting through the waves would be easier. At least she wouldn't freeze to death.

All the guys started laughing, Waldo the loudest.

"What's so funny?" Molly demanded.

"You have the suit on backward. The zipper goes in the back."

"Could they make this any harder?" she said, yanking and pulling the neoprene back down over her hips to start over.

"You got that right, girl. The most exhausting part of the whole day is getting in and out of your wet suit," Buzz complained, even though his body was long and lean and his suit fit him like a glove.

Molly grabbed the back fastener and yanked the zipper

up in fits and starts until she was finally zipped in. But when she had it on right, it was way too baggy across the chest. Waldo started laughing again, this time even louder. "Looks like AJ's got bigger man-boobs than Molly does girl ones. Hey, Molls, maybe you should wear it backward. It fits better."

All the guys laughed except for Flea who, like Molly, was unamused by derogatory references to size. Molly squared off in front of Waldo.

"Speaking of fit, Waldo, I understand that your whole package would fit into a lipstick case," she said.

"Where did you hear that?" Waldo asked, offended.

"I read it in the girls' locker room. First stall to the right as you walk through the door," Molly said, adding another lie to her list.

"Have you even been in the girls' locker room, Molly?" Riki asked.

"Hey, he started it," Molly insisted, and turned to Waldo. "Do not and I repeat *do not* get into a pissin' contest with me over matters related to size. Because that's where I draw the line."

"Listen up, girlfriend, the right to insult us is an earned privilege. And so far, we are unimpressed," Riki said, tougher than any of the guys.

They grabbed their boards, leaving her alone, as they

headed into the surf. Instead of joining them in the water, she wandered over to Duke, who was sitting on the sand, savoring a cup of black coffee from the 7-Eleven. Duke disapproved of fancy coffee drinks; he bragged that he was the only one left in Hermosa who had not crossed over to the latte. Much more subdued than usual, Molly plopped down on the sand beside him. After a while, he asked, "You going in the water today, Molly?"

"I have a headache," she answered, too intimidated to even give it a try.

"Too bad, because it looks like a nice morning to be on the water."

"Are you gonna lower my grade if I sit this one out?"

Duke smiled. "You mean you get a grade for this class?"

They sat side by side on the sand in silence, observing the others, who were catching dozens and dozens of waves. Bored, Molly scooped out a hole in the sand with her feet so deep, she could have buried herself up to her waist.

That night, Molly posted in her blog.

It didn't really matter if Duke gave me a grade or not because the fact is, I had already failed more than his class. I had failed myself. Today I felt the call of the water and I allowed myself to be intimidated by the Dawn Patrol, masters of ridicule who hunted in a pack.

Molly wiped her cheek with the back of her hand,

realizing that if she had been writing in an old-fashioned journal with pen in hand, her pages would be stained with tears. Angry, she made a vow to herself to never to let their laughter or teasing keep her chained to the shore when the water beckoned.

FIVE

THE FOLLOWING TUESDAY, A FOG BANK SAT JUST OFF THE COAST AT CATALINA, THE sun burning through to a crisp blue sky. Milling around on the sand, board under her arm, Molly resolved that she would not only go into the water, she would make it past the breakers. As she scanned the shore, searching for the best point of entry, she saw a harbor patrol boat approaching from the south. The boat idled and pulled close into shore, and a lifeguard in a red swimsuit jumped off the stern and bodysurfed in to the shore.

"Hey, it's Archie," Waldo said, recognizing the lifeguard. "Wonder why he's swimming in?"

"Maybe there's a fast break firin' on eighteenth," AJ hoped.

"Or could be a shark sighting," Kai said, pulling a can of wax out of his surf bag.

Molly's ears perked up at the mere mention of a shark.

Perhaps she would sit out one more day and wait until Thursday to actually go into the water.

The man emerged from the water. All the kids recognized Michael Archiletta, affectionately known as Archie. He was a section guard for the L.A. County lifeguards and in his spare time, he worked with an organization that served as the primary responder for sick and injured marine mammals. In fact, Archie had been the one who had suggested that Duke, his old surfing buddy from back in the day, apply for the Surf Ed. instructor job.

He and Duke embraced each other the way macho men do with one strong arm over the shoulder, one quick, hard pound on the back. Although they were close to the same age, Archie looked much younger. He was a little taller than Duke and had a hard, well-toned body—not exactly a six-pack, but as close to one as anyone over forty got.

"Waves suck today," he said solemnly.

"For sure," Duke answered, laughing with the others. "And thanks for swimming in your personal, firsthand report. But you could have called in surf conditions on your cell."

"I know, but it was a good excuse to get in the water. And it felt damn good," Archie said, shaking the water out of his longish blond hair like a shaggy golden retriever fresh out of the water. He gestured to Molly. "Who's the new grommet?"

"That's Molly Browne, and it's Browne with an 'e'. She's from Texas and she has potential."

"Potential" was code for the girl who didn't know squat about surfing. Frustrated with Duke for letting an inexperienced surfer into the class, Archie commented, "Please tell me that she at least knows how to swim."

"Well, she hasn't drowned yet," Duke said optimistically.

Archie shook his head and, before heading into the ocean for the boat, he offered one last piece of advice to the grommet: "Try to stay out of trouble."

"That's the plan," Molly said.

As Archie dove under the first set of breakers, Molly turned to Duke. "I thought I'd put the board in the water today."

"Good. The conditions are perfect today for learning how to paddle out."

"Got any pointers?"

"It's a good board. You'll be fine."

"Could you be a little more specific? Like tell me how I get to that place called 'fine,'" Molly said.

"Hey Kai, wanna teach the grommet how to paddle out?"

Kai was waxing his board nearby, making little knobs of traction. He looked up, annoyed. "Not really."

"Do it, anyway," Duke replied.

"Thanks, brah, you know how to brighten my morning!" Kai said.

Molly followed Kai to the shoreline and it was difficult to tell who was more uncomfortable with the student-teacher setup, Molly or Kai.

"I hope you're a fast learner," Kai said.

"You're under no obligation. I can figure it out on my own," Molly said, offended.

"Look, when Duke asks you to do something, you do it. So let's just get this over with."

They walked her board out into knee-deep water. Duke was right: It was a perfect day to learn; there wasn't much current or undertow. Kai showed her how to balance her body weight along the center of the board and to raise her feet slightly off the end. He taught her to reach out with one arm at a time and stroke her way through the water, keeping it even and smooth. She had good form and she looked very promising up until the first wave rolled over her. She slipped too far back on the board, causing it to pop out in front of her like a torpedo.

Molly actually made it past the breakers in only six attempts. Her pride, Kai's knowledge, and another flat day on the water proved to be a successful combination. Having officially made it to the lineup, Molly was quite content to sit on her board and roll with the swells. She found it infinitely more fun to dangle her feet in the water than dig her feet into the sand. With no good waves for Kai to chase, they drifted in silence for a very long time. She studied her reluctant teacher out of the corner of her eye and noticed a scar on his left side, which she asked about.

"A hammerhead shark tried to take a piece of me."

Molly looked down at the ominously murky waters, imagining all sorts of predatory sea creatures lurking beneath the surface, poised to attack. Just to be safe, she pulled her legs up out of the water onto her board, explaining to the other guys who paddled out to the lineup that she had no intention of becoming breakfast for a shark.

Waldo laughed. "You're not big enough for breakfast; you'd be more like a mid-morning snack."

"Did we not recently have a conversation about making references to size?" Molly asked.

"Yeah, back off, a-hole," Flea said, without any rancor. "Don't worry, Molly, sharks are predators. They go after the old or weak."

"And sea lions, which is their favorite food." Buzz added. "The problem is, of course, that a surfer in a black wet suit closely resembles a sea lion."

"Always surf with a partner," AJ said, the last to join the

lineup. "It cuts the chances of your being eaten by a shark in half."

"They're just jerking your chain, Molly. Most sharks don't attack without provocation," Flea said.

"Except for the great white," Kai said reverently.

They were all silent for a moment, paying homage to the mighty beast of the sea.

"Last summer, they caught a great white shark near the pier," Kai offered. "He was eighteen feet long, weighed almost two tons."

Molly gazed at the pier that jutted into the water, mentally measuring the distance from this break. It was only a couple hundred yards, at best—way too close for comfort. "What did they do with the shark?"

"They let her go."

"The freed a killer shark into these waters?"

"Yes."

"Where we swim and surf?"

"Yeah."

"That is just so wrong!"

Kai shook his head, exasperated. "This isn't Texas, Molly. This is California. We try to work with nature."

"Well, so do we. But when my dad found a rattler sleeping in my closet, he did not call the SPCA. He grabbed a twenty-two and shot the sonofabitch. How can you justify letting a known killer loose into your own backyard?"

"Okay, let's start with, it's *their* ocean. We're just here on a day pass. Now, can we stop the chatter and just enjoy the day?"

"Who made you the wave police?" Molly asked.

"You know what I like best about Riki?" Kai asked.

"What?" Molly asked, confused by his sudden change of subject.

"She's not too chatty. And most girls are too chatty in the water," Kai observed pointedly.

"Hey, I'm not the one who's been doing all the talking," Molly said defensively.

A natural peacemaker, Flea interjected himself into the conversation. "Sooner or later, Molls, you're going to have an encounter of the ocean kind. The first one should be under more controlled circumstances. Catch the next wave in."

Grateful to be on the cement stretch of pier overlooking the shark-infested waters, instead of in them, Molly followed Flea to the end of the pier to a funky aquarium, affectionately known as the Roundhouse. No bigger than a large apartment and requiring only a two-dollar donation, the research lab housed a touching tank of tide pool animals and a larger tank. Flea waved to the young docent on the second floor who was posting children's artwork of sea creatures on the walls. "Hey, Flea, what's up? How's the surf?"

"Worse than bad. Mind if I introduce the new girl to The Porker?"

"Knock yourself out, brah."

In one of the larger tanks were half a dozen fish common to the Santa Monica Bay, including a scary-looking moray eel and a giant lobster. Molly and Flea climbed on the viewing platform above the aquarium looking down into the waters. He pulled a pole net across the sandy bottom floor of the tank and scooped up an odd-looking fish with a tan body and small brown spots and a large, blocky, piglike head (hence his name). The Porker was three feet long; he had a dorsal spine and large pectoral fins. He moved sluggishly, which made him easy to catch. Flea lifted the fish out of the tank and held him in his arms, offering him to Molly, who was a bit put off because the Porker was decidedly unattractive.

"Go ahead, touch him. He likes to be petted. But watch out for the spine. It has sharp edges."

Molly ran her hand from the head of the fish to its tail. It felt rough, like sandpaper, but when she changed directions, running her hand back from tail to head, the Porker was smooth as silk.

"What kind of fish is it?" Molly asked.

"It's not a fish," Flea replied. "It's a Horn shark."

"Does he bite?" Molly asked, trying to sound casual.

"Only if you piss him off," Flea explained. "Kinda like Kai. And if you'd stop trying to piss him off, you might discover he's okay."

"Kai's a prick, but I kind of like this guy," Molly said, patting the top of the Porker's head.

Flea shrugged and released the Horn shark back into the tank. He drifted back down to the sandy bottom.

They stepped out of the Roundhouse into bright sunlight. The early morning fog bank had rolled away, the outline of Catalina Island crystal clear on the horizon. "Just remember that if you're going to swim with the sharks, make sure you don't cut yourself before you plunge into the water," Flea said as they walked down the pier. Molly looked across the sunlit dappled waters below and wondered if Flea was referring to the Porker or to Kai.

SIX

**EVERY TUESDAY AND THURSDAY DURING
THE REST OF SEPTEMBER, MOLLY AWOKE**
at the crack of dawn with one goal: to get her board out
beyond the breakers and to make it back in at the end of
Surf Ed. class without dying. Thus far, she had been amazingly successful. Her timing had improved, and she hadn't
torpedoed since, well, last Thursday. But in between making
it past the breakers and getting back in, Molly found her
true calling as a water girl.

The best part of her day was joining the lineup with the
other surfers, facing the ocean, judging the arrival of each
new set. But unlike Riki and the guys who were actually out
there to surf, she was perfectly content to sit on her board and
watch the swells roll in. It gave her time to think and to reflect.
While the others searched for the perfect wave, she searched
for plausible reasons as to why her mother left her father, why
she had decided to move to California, why Kai irritated

Molly so much, and why Andrea had taken such an interest in her. Once she realized that Duke wasn't going to kick her out of the class, she was quite content to get PE credit for sitting on her board. She had no desire to fly down the face of the wave. In Molly's opinion, surfing was superfluous to the pure experience of just being on the water.

Today as she stood on the shore zipping her wet suit, she marveled at the way the color of the water changed with the conditions, ranging from the lightest sky blue to turquoise to teal to deep violet to steely gray. She had read once that the Eskimos had over a hundred words for "snow." She wondered if the Chumash Indians who first settled these California shores had had as many words for ocean.

Duke interrupted her reverie. "Molls, I think it's time for you to actually take a stab at surfing. And the first step to standing up on your board is to figure out if you're a natural foot or a goofy-foot surfer."

"Thanks, but I'm happy the way things are. In my opinion the best part of surfing is getting out beyond the breakers and sitting on your board," Molly said.

"How would you know? You haven't surfed yet," Kai snapped.

"Shut up," Molly snapped back.

Duke came to Molly's defense. "I have spent hundreds and hundreds of hours sitting out on my board, staring at the horizon, just letting life unfold. And none of it was wasted time."

Duke motioned Flea over and asked him if he would show Molly how to pop up on a board. Molly started to protest, but Duke insisted: "Let him give you a few pointers, just in case you decide to give it a try. Because when it comes to the pop-up, Flea's the man."

Flea basked in Duke's praise. As did they all.

"Hey, Flea, your ass crack's showing," Waldo called out. If Duke singled any of the guys out for commendation, one of the others would quickly jump in and cut the chosen one down to size. It was an unwritten code.

Flea hiked up his shorts and shot Waldo the finger, only pretending to be annoyed.

"Hey, I'm just covering your back—so to speak," Waldo called out, teasing.

Ignoring Waldo, Flea laid his board down in the sand because it was easier to demonstrate on dry land. He showed Molly the correct position, lying down flat on his board, straight out on his stomach. He placed his hands by his shoulders, board width apart. And then in a nanosecond he snapped up to a crouched standing position, his left foot forward in one fluid, graceful movement. Flea was, of course, a natural foot surfer.

Molly lay on her board, stomach down. She placed her

arms shoulder-width apart and tried to mimic his smooth move. But she could only raise herself halfway up; the other half of her seemed glued to the board.

"Try arching your back and pushing up as your feet come up beneath you," he suggested.

She gave it another try but with no more success than her first attempt.

"You don't have much upper body strength, do you?"

"Do push-ups every night, Molly," Riki suggested as she strolled by, toting her board under one arm, unfettered, like she was carrying a teeny beaded bag instead of a thirty-pound long board.

"Said the queen of the push-up bra," Molly said, barely under breath.

Overhearing, Riki dropped her chin and zeroed in with a look meant to level her. "I do two hundred one-arm push-ups with a clap every other night. My brother's a U.S. Navy SEAL and even he can't keep up with me."

Determined to prove herself, Molly muscled herself up and this time she managed to scramble to her knees. She wobbled and stood up awkwardly. Flea shook his head sadly. If she was this tentative on solid ground, he hated to imagine her attempting the same move in more liquid and less forgiving surroundings. "It's one move, Molly, not two. Surfing on your knees is a bad habit that's hard to break."

Once more she tried, and once more she failed, falling on her board with a soft thud. Flea shook his head in frustration. "I thought this would be easy for you. Big guys are the ones who generally have trouble mastering this move, but you should pop up like bread out of a toaster."

Waldo rode a wave all the way into shore, bailed, and came out, waving his arms. "Yo, Flea, it's totally cranking on the outside."

"I think that's enough for today, don't you?" Molly asked.

Flea considered. He knew that Molly could use a few more tries on the safe sand, but the day's possibility on the water was slipping away from him. A light fog rolled in, foiling the sunny day promised earlier by a clear sunrise. The line between the horizon and the sea blurred into one large canvas of gray. Molly got off her board and stood by him. Together, they faced the shorebreak. The draw of the ocean was powerful for both of them, and each was tempted to forgo the lesson, but for different reasons. Molly desperately wanted to ditch the dry land drills and paddle out to the place where she could get lost in her thoughts. Flea longed to drop down the face of a well-shaped four-footer. Out of the corner of his eye he caught a glimpse of Molly gazing out to sea. For half a minute, he studied her face unnoticed and he saw something in her expression. Something she had not yet fully realized herself. She was a kindred spirit. She didn't need to practice on land. Everything she needed to know, she would learn in the water. By herself. And in her own time.

"What are you thinking about?" she asked.

"About something Kai once said."

"What's that?"

"The water runs through us," Flea explained.

"What does that mean?"

"That water connects us; it's our common bond. And it means that the lesson's over for today. Woohoo!" Flea screamed as he rushed the white water, knees akimbo.

Molly waited for a lull before making her initial charge, and made a more cautious, studied entrance into the water than the upstart Flea. After only three attempts she made it past the breakers, arriving to the lineup just as Flea took off on his first ride of the day, releasing thousands of powerful feel-good chemicals into his brain as he dipped into the barrel. Smiling, Molly sat up on her board and rolled with the swells, confirming once again that there was more than one way to have fun on the water.

That evening, Molly opened up her MySpace page and checked to see if she had any new comments from her top eight friends, which in and of itself was a misnomer. While other kids spent hours whittling down their mega-list of friends down to the privileged few, Molly still had four vacancies. Oh, and one of her top eight was her father. How embarrassing was that? When she first added him to the list, he insisted on the screen name no.1Dad. She pleaded with him to change it to something less identifiable and more hip; she didn't want anyone to know that she was padding her top eight with relatives. He changed his screen name to lubbocklad, which he thought was extremely clever, and posted comments on her page every other day.

Molly's own screen name was sexysax05. She chose "sexy" because if you put "sexy" in your online identity, you were guaranteed a certain amount of attention from the get-go, and "sax" for "saxophone" because it was always smart to wrap your screen name around your main passion, and she lopped a 05 at the end because adding numbers made you sound important, like James Bond.

Molly was interrupted by an instant message: "Bored with bio. Come over at 9:22 for wardrobe make-over."

Molly didn't need to check the screen name to see who it was from. No one but Andrea would ask someone to hang out at 9:22. Andrea signed off QTvp (which stood for cutie vice president).

• • •

"I'm going over to Andrea's for a little while," Molly called to her mom as she grabbed her house keys out of her backpack.

Almost dressed for work, Lynette was searching the living room for her missing shoe. Because she had no seniority, Lynette had to work the graveyard shift, from ten at night to six in the morning, forcing her into an upside-down schedule. Lynette went to bed when Molly was waking up; she was sleeping when Molly got home from school. And on Tuesdays and Thursdays when Molly had Surf Ed., Molly left before her mother even got home. The only real time they had together was the evening meal, and even that was strained.

"Where does Andrea live?" Lynette asked. "Is it safe to walk, or do you want me to drive you?"

"Mom, don't worry about it, okay? She lives on the Strand, so it's not like I have to cross Sepulveda or anything," Molly said.

"How long will you be gone?" Lynette asked, discovering her shoe behind a pillow on the couch, left there when she'd slipped it off while watching television.

"Not long," Molly said evasively.

"How long is not long?" Lynette continued, pressuring.

"I won't be late," Molly answered, getting more annoyed by the minute. "Trust me, I'm not sure I even like her enough to stay much past an hour."

"Is something wrong with her?" Lynette asked.

"No, it's just that she's not really my friend. I'm her—" Molly said, adding, "study partner."

Molly was not about to tell her mom, or anybody else, for that matter, that she was Andrea's special project.

"Well, I guess it's okay for you to go as long as you're back by curfew," Lynette said, putting on her best concerned-parent voice.

"Mom, I don't have a curfew because I don't need a curfew because I never go anywhere."

Which was not entirely true. Molly often left the trailer after her mother left for work. She did not, however, *go anywhere* specific. She wandered through downtown Hermosa, peeking in the clubs, looking in the store windows. But Molly felt that if it was okay for Lynette to be less than forthcoming about her own personal life—the breakup of her marriage, and the impending divorce—then Molly was allowed to have her own secrets as well. The real problem between mother and daughter was never what they said to each other; it was what they kept from each other. The unspoken between them was as vast as the ocean a mere two blocks away.

Molly looked at the reflection of her new made-over self in the mirror in Andrea's walk-in closet, which approximated in square footage Molly's entire living and dining area. Andrea spent most of the fifty-three minutes of their allotted hang-time accessorizing Molly with borrowed bits and pieces from Andrea's closet: a string of pearls, a ruffled blouse, a wide-brimmed fedora. Andrea was trying to create a look for Molly that said "serious yet romantic," one that would present her to the world as an artist, a musician. And while Andrea was not one of those girls who spent hours combing the latest fashion magazines, she did believe that the physical presentation of oneself was as important as one's club titles. "You need to make sure that what you look like on the outside is a true representation of who you are on the inside. It's like choosing your screen name, which is way more important than what you say. And if you don't believe me, just see how much respect you get in a chat room if you call yourself 'phat-teen,' even if you spell it with a 'ph' instead of an 'f.'"

Molly smiled. For the first time she felt an honest connection with Andrea. They chatted easily for the next ten minutes and agreed that posting your screen name on an Internet site was tantamount to putting up a super-size bill-board advertisement on the highway. A screen name announced to the world whom you were and what you were about; it was the first impression you made in a chat room and could be the last impression if you chose badly. Molly told a story to illustrate the point.

"I knew this guy in Lubbock, a total *wangster*, you know—white gangster—who was going for an ultracool combo of Snoop Dogg and P. Diddy. So he chose the screen name 'poop.doggie'. And, of course, everybody called him 'Dog-shit' after that."

Andrea doubled over with laughter, but Molly, seeing that it was already ten thirty-three, excused herself to change back into her own clothes. When she returned, blouse and hat in hand, Andrea told her she could take all of it home, including the pearls because they made her look like a true California girl and not a Texas transplant. Molly gingerly placed the hat, the blouse, and the pearls on Andrea's bed.

"We have an old saying in Texas: 'Pasting feathers together does not make a duck.' I do appreciate your wanting to help me fit in at Beach. But the truth is, I'm not cool enough to be a California girl. And I don't want to be anybody's special project. But I'd like for us to be friends."

It was a brave move on Molly's part, especially because they had been getting on so well. But that was precisely why Molly felt the need to even the playing field. Andrea was smart and she could be funny, but if they were ever going to be friends, they had to move beyond rescuer and victim; they needed a more equal footing. Andrea hesitated; she was not particularly fond of equal relationships and she hated in principle the idea of dropping a project halfway through to completion. She reluctantly agreed, but with the caveat that if they were going to be friends, then they had to tell each other everything. Molly had never heard that particular rule before, but then she didn't have a plethora of friends, either.

"What do you want to know?" Molly wondered, figuring it must be important if not earth-shattering since Andrea was already five minutes past the allotment for her study break. Andrea pressed her to tell her about the guys in Surf Ed., admitting that she'd been secretly fascinated by this group because they seemed so beyond the rules of high school, especially Kai.

Molly told her about seeing him for the first time at the pier and how he had yelled at the crazy skateboard rider in her defense. "I was impressed. I thought he was really warm and compassionate."

"And hot . . ."

"Well, yeah. He was hot."

"He *is* hot," Andrea said, correcting her.

"Turns out he's also totally self-centered. If it gets in the way of his perfect day or his perfect wave, he can't be bothered," Molly said.

"God, Molly, you say 'self-centered' like it was a bad thing," Andrea said.

Molly looked at her, wondering, "Are you crushing on him?"

"Oh no, he's so not my type. I want a guy with more ambition, somebody who's headed for the Ivy League. I don't think Kai has the grades or the inclination. Besides, I heard he was hooked up with that Riki person."

"I think Riki hooks up with just about everybody. But she seems to be with Waldo now. But this much I do know: Kai respects her."

"But she's a slut."

"True, but he likes the fact that she's not too chatty."

Andrea shrugged and made a mental note to keep small talk to a minimum.

After leaving Andrea's mansion on the Strand, Molly avoided the busy pier and took a less crowded and more direct route home. She was worn out and ready to call it a night. She slipped into the trailer park and as she walked by the first row of trailers, she heard a familiar voice call out her name. She turned and saw Duke, sitting on his front stoop and nursing a beer, so she stopped to chat.

"I was wondering, just in case I ever need to know: How can you tell if you're natural footed or just plain goofy?"

"If you were to skid across an ice pond, which foot would you put in front?" Duke asked.

"I have no idea. There hasn't been water, much less ice, in Lubbock Lake for tens of thousands of years," Molly said.

"Too bad, because the skid test is the most reliable way to tell which foot you should bring forward when you pop up to surf."

He told her to stand with her left foot forward and to rock back and forth. "How does that feel?" he asked.

"Okay, I guess."

Duke took a long sip of his beer. "Try it with your right foot forward. What about that?"

"It feels better. Why?"

"Well, if I were you, I'd wear my leash on my left foot, just in case."

He finished the bottle and tossed it into a recycling bin nearby. It was already overflowing with empty beer bottles, and trash pick-up was three days away. Molly thanked him for the advice. For the board. And especially for not kicking her out of Surf Ed. on that very first day.

"And I hope this doesn't sound rude, but is there a reason you're being so nice to me?" Molly asked.

"Do you think there has to be a reason for someone to be nice to you?"

"Most of the time, yes."

"Well, I agree with you. When one person is nice to another, there's almost always a reason."

"So will you share yours with me?"

He looked at her and considered.

"No, it's too late for a really long story, and I haven't had enough to drink," Duke said as he stood and walked up the steps to his trailer.

Duke believed that timing was everything. He knew that someday he would tell Molly about the book that had saved his life, and her connection to it. Someday, when the time was right. But not tonight.

SEVEN

ALTHOUGH MOLLY REMAINED A DEDICATED NIGHT PERSON, SHE ALSO BECAME FOR TWO days every week a born-again morning person. And after two months of early morning sessions in the water, the joy of Molly's new routine was indescribable, although she was squeezed for time to blog. But tonight as a Halloween harvest moon rose in her window, Molly opened her laptop to begin a new blog entry, and her emotions poured out.

There are days on the water when a wispy fog settles in, tinting the water as gray as the sky, so that there is no longer the delineation between them. You cannot tell where the ocean ends and the heavens begin. And that is when Hermosa reminds me most of Lubbock. A lot of people might wonder what the scenic appeal of the Texas Panhandle is. In one word, it is sky—so big that it goes it on endlessly, like the ocean in a light mist. The smooth line of the horizon on the Plains is like an ocean in the doldrums. My dad used to say that in Lubbock, you could see all the way to the beginning of time. He loved Lubbock. Not my mom. She never cared for it, although she never said anything bad about it either, because Mom just doesn't say anything bad about anything. But in her opinion, there wasn't much to admire in Plain country except sky, and she was not a sky person.

Molly paused from her midnight musings to remember the first time she had left sky country. When she was ten, her parents moved to Austin for a year. Lynette loved everything about that city, deep in the heart of Texas—the rolling hills, the lakes, and the music that drifted out of the downtown clubs on Sixth Street. The family settled into a rambling stone house on the south side of town with a deep front yard full of hundred-year-old oak trees. Their branches hung so low and were so dense that the street was not visible from the front porch. It was like living in a forest. Lynette bought baskets full of begonias and hung them, draping the trees with pots of colors. That was what Molly remembered most about living in hill country: the trees in the front yard.

That and the day they were gone.

She and her mother had spent the day swimming in the refreshingly chilly waters of Barton Springs. They returned home at dusk as the last of the trucks were pulling away. Her father had hired a tree service to cut down every

single tree in the front yard. Lynette burst into tears, sobbing and screaming hysterically like a madwoman, demanding to know how he could have done such a horrible thing.
He told her that he had felt trapped, that he needed a clear
view of things.

I don't know which upset me more—Molly typed—*the
loss of my forest, or seeing my mother so completely unhinged.
Shortly afterward, we moved back to Lubbock and our old life.
Neither of them ever mentioned the tree cutting incident
again. Our new front yard was uncluttered; nothing blocked
our magnificent view of thunderheads when the spring storms
blew in. And we were much happier in the western reaches of
the state. Who needs hills and lakes and water when you have
sky? At least I thought we were happier. And although my parents never mentioned that Austin evening again, sometimes I
wonder if those trees held the secret to the beginning of the end
of their marriage.*

Molly was the first to arrive on the beach the next day. She
sipped her double-shot latte from Java Boy and scanned the
horizon. The wind was blowing gently across the blue-green
waters, and the surf was breaking perfect four-footers close to
the beach. She watched a lone surfer rip the line, mesmerized
by the play of light across the surface of the growing swells,
and the rhythmic roar and hiss of foam as it rolled shoreward.

One by one, the group onshore grew until it was thirty strong, all waiting for Duke's arrival. He crested the dune and waved them in, and a parade of wet suits and boards hit the water. Molly paddled out and took her place on the outside of the lineup, far from the breaking waves. She watched Riki turn in and catch the first wave of the day. But the waves were much steeper and faster than they'd been all week, and she didn't adjust. She stood up too fast and buried the nose of the surfboard in the water. She was barely able to bail from the ride before she torpedoed. As she rejoined the lineup, Kai told her, "Angle on the takeoff as you drop into the wave."

Riki took Kai's advice and ripped the line on her next ride. Molly had noted in her short time on the water that the others not only depended on one another but learned from one another. Maybe that's what Flea meant when he said "the water runs through us."

For half an hour Molly rolled with the swells and while the others surfed the beautiful break with varying degrees of success, she got lost in her own thoughts. She found it odd the things that suddenly popped into her head when she was on the water, random disconnected thoughts like static on a radio. But occasionally something worthwhile would emerge, something worth considering, fodder for her blog.

"HEADS UP, MOLLY!"

Molly broke from her reverie just in time to see one of the better sets of the day roll in. The wave was breaking on the far outside, so instead of Molly being last, she was suddenly catapulted by King Neptune, into the first position in the lineup.

A chorus of encouragement arose from the Dawn Patrol as they screamed for her to "Go for it," "Take off," and "Don't waste it." Molly flipped over onto her stomach as the wave crested. The wave was steep and formed more typically like those found in Hawaii than in Southern California.

Molly headed down the face of the wave, careening toward certain disaster. A voice inside her head was screaming that death was imminent, and then something remarkable happened. That nagging voice miraculously hushed, and her body developed a mind of its own. Pulsing through her muscles, nerves, and bloodstream, it shouted, "Let's take a real ride on this crazy surf machine!"

And before the sensible voice inside her head had the opportunity for a rebuttal, Molly popped up on her board.

Standing at the water's edge, Duke shaded his eyes and squinted to get a better look. He was not disappointed, nor was he surprised. It was just as he'd thought, exactly what he'd expected. Molly was a goofy-foot grommet.

She sailed right foot forward into the wave. She felt

herself falling, flying briefly as she planed across the face of the wave for eight exquisite seconds.

Eight life-changing seconds.

One-eighth of a monumental moment.

Nothing she had ever done in her whole life felt half this good. Not even making out with Dalton Reece her freshman year in the parking lot of the Dairy Queen after it closed.

She ended her brief but memorable ride with a monster wipeout. She pearled and was dragged under the water, pulled along by the board. Hammered by the whitewash, she literally washed up on the beach, her board flipping and flopping in the churning foam. She scrambled to her feet in the ankle-deep water, spitting out flotsam and jetsam. Her hair was plastered to the side of her head like some weird version of a faux hawk. But she didn't care. She pulled her leash and got control of her unruly board, wild-eyed with wonder.

"So how was it?" Duke asked, already knowing the answer.

Breathless and awed, Molly could not find the words to describe what she felt. She stood there, grinning and shaking her head.

In one-eighth of a minute, Molly had completely turned around. She would no longer be content to just roll with the swells. She would never again complain about getting up early to catch a wave. She had found her place in the lineup. To put it simply: Molly was hooked for life.

Flea, Waldo, Kai, AJ, and Buzz jogged through the shorebreak to check on her.

"Did you see me ride that monster wave?" Molly asked.

"Whoa, there, girlfriend. Let's be real. It was steep, but it was only four feet. And you stayed up for all of eight seconds," Waldo said, soundly putting her in her place.

"Yeah, but it was a great eight seconds," Molly said, smiling impishly. "And from what I hear, Waldo, eight seconds is about all you can stay up too."

The others laughed as the sun broke out from behind the cloud bank.

"Not bad for a goofy-foot," Kai commented.

Molly replayed the pop-up in her head and realized that he was right. She had surfed with her right foot forward and it had felt as natural as walking. But she worried that being goofy-footed somehow diminished her stature in the surfing world. Kai placed a reassuring hand on her shoulder.

"Nothing's wrong with being a goofy-foot. Tom Carroll was one of the most powerful surfers of all time and he surfed right foot forward," Kai said, snatching his board up and heading back into the water to take advantage of one more ride before class was over.

Surprised, Molly turned to Flea for confirmation. "Am I crazy or was he being nice to me?"

Flea shrugged. "Yes to both. You're making headway, Molls, but don't get too full of yourself. You may have surfed. But you're not a surfer. Not yet."

He smiled and added, "But you're definitely on your way."

Most days, Kai gave Waldo and Riki rides home to shower before school. But today, because Molly was standing right next to Riki and obviously on foot, it seemed awkward not to include her. So Kai offered her a ride home, one more indication that she was making headway into the Dawn Patrol. Molly hesitated, unsure if she wanted the other kids to know that she lived in the trailer park, a fact she had kept thus far from everyone except Duke. In the end, she decided that the possibility of discovery was worth the risk.

Flea, Waldo, Kai, Riki, and Molly chugged up the soft sand to the lot where Kai's beat-up red Volvo wagon was parked. The front bumper was dented and crooked and the passenger door was taxicab yellow, having been replaced after a collision with a discard from a wrecking yard. Kai's mom had been willing to foot the bill to have the door repainted to match the car, but Kai never got around to taking the car into the body shop. He'd spend hours buffing out the slightest ding on his board, but he didn't take the same pride in his on-land vehicle as he did his ride on water.

Molly loved the car immediately; she thought it had character. Kai lay his board down first and, after putting a towel on top so he wouldn't scratch it, strapped Molly's board on top of his. Molly was surprised by how much this simple gesture moved her; the care he took with her board was sweet.

"So where do you live, Molly?" asked Kai as he and Waldo bungeed the other boards to the second rack.

"You can just drop me off at Valley and Pier," she said, planning to bail half a block from the turnoff to the trailer park.

As they neared the intersection, Kai slowed down. And since there were no houses, no apartment buildings in sight, he asked what street she lived on.

Molly made a mental note to thumb through her mother's Thomas Bros. map of Los Angeles and locate a street name near the trailer park that she could use in just these cases because you can't randomly make up names for streets or landmarks in a town that was only one square mile big. "Marineland Park Drive," she answered, trapped into revealing where she lived.

"Ohmigod, do you live in the trailer park?" asked Riki, who

was sandwiched between Flea and Waldo in the backseat.

"Yeah, but it's just temporary, until they finish building our house on the Strand," Molly said. Lying about her imaginary home under imaginary construction to Andrea had been easy, but lying to the Dawn Patrol made her uneasy.

"That is so cool," Riki said, sounding almost jealous.

"Yeah, living on the Strand is going to be awesome," Molly said, conjuring up a vision of Andrea's three-story, eight-thousand-square-foot beach "cottage" with its floor-to-ceiling ocean views.

"No, I meant the trailer park is cool."

"Totally," Buzz chimed in, adjusting his shades.

Molly was stunned. She couldn't believe that California kids considered a trailer park cool. In Texas, a trailer park was the quintessential wrong-side-of-the-tracks address. One of the star basketball players at Garfield High had lived in one and even his varsity letterman's jacket couldn't cover his shame. She felt certain that when a tornado leveled his double-wide, he had been secretly relieved to move into an apartment, which although smaller had infinitely more cachet than a trailer mounted on concrete blocks. What Molly hadn't realized was the importance of location in California real estate, especially proximity to the water. If you lived close to the beach, it didn't matter if your house was made out of tin. You could even live out of your car and be considered cool as long as it was permanently parked near the sand.

Molly thanked Kai for the ride, climbed out of the car, and unhooked her surfboard from the hood. She waved as Kai pulled away, his tires resting so low from the weight of the boards and three backseat passengers that it looked as if he might scrape the bottom on the dip in the road. He whipped into a U-turn, and that's when she saw the sign for the first time. Scripted on the driver's side of Kai's Volvo version of a woody surf wagon in bold capital letters were the words MATH TUTORING. Underneath was Kai's phone number. Bit by bit, all her preconceptions—about the trailer park, about the group, about Kai—were being challenged. Was nothing in California as it appeared to be?

"I talked to Riki and found out Kai's taking precalc," Molly told Andrea later that week in jazz band.

"And American history AP," Andrea added. "Plus, he got a perfect score on the math section of his Plan test."

"How do you know that?"

"I have my sources," Andrea said, smiling. But what Molly didn't know at that time was that she was one of them.

EIGHT

**THAT EIGHT-SECOND RIDE TURNED MOLLY'S
LIFE AROUND. IT TOOK THREE MORE WEEKS**
of bail-outs and capsizes before she actually stood up on her
board for longer than she had on her first pop-up. She
became the first to arrive (not counting Kai) and the last to
leave Surf Ed. After school, she paddled her board out
beyond the breakers to practice, and in the evenings she
surfed the web for sites that had tips on riding waves, studying the techniques of the masters. And after she logged off
her computer, she hit the floor for a hundred push-ups. But
sheer desire on land did not translate into proficiency on
the water. She wiped out so many times that she began to
feel like she was on the permanent spin cycle of an aged
washing machine. From his place in the sand, Duke continued to give her pointers—nothing major, just small
things, one or two hints at a time. His goals for her were
modest. He wasn't trying to turn her into a competitive

surfer; he was simply dedicated to showing her how to get the most out her time in the water. And she soaked up everything he said like sun on a winter day.

By the beginning of November, Molly could not only make it through the breakers, she could surf three-footers. She was lucky because the surf conditions in September and October had been mild with no strong undertow, no pesky rips pulling swimmers out to sea. The other guys complained about the benign conditions—Buzz, especially, who could find fault with even a perfect day. But Molly made the most of this period of grace, improving her skill daily, even as Waldo and the others longed for a winter storm to bring on the tropical swells. Because she spent more time trying to catch waves instead of sitting on her board, she had less time to spend on reflection. If her inner life suffered and her blog drifted into dormancy, she more than made up for the decline in conversations with her own self with the thrill of flying down the face of a wave.

"I'm leaving in fifteen minutes, Molly," Lynette called out on a Wednesday evening. "Is there anything you need before I go?"

Lynette knocked on the door to Molly's bedroom. Unlocked and slightly ajar, it pushed open easily. Molly stood in front of the mirror over her vanity, wearing a bikini top and rolled-down boxer shorts, staring at her reflection with the kind of detachment usually reserved for strangers.

"Look at me. Do you see something different?" Molly asked. Her voice was distant, dreamy.

Lynette studied Molly, trying to pick up some subtle difference in her daughter. She noticed beads of sweat on the back of Molly's neck; her face was flushed. "Are you sick? Do you have a fever?"

Molly had completed her nightly exercise routine just minutes before her mother had stepped in her room, which was why she was sweating. Frustrated that her mother had not noticed the dramatic changes in her body, like the ripples of definition on her stomach, Molly closed her fist and flexed her arm muscles, posing like an athlete. "I've got gunboats," Molly said, pointing out the definition in her biceps.

Lynette smiled, and her shoulders relaxed with relief. "You're a beautiful girl, Molly."

"Don't say that," Molly said, annoyed.

"Why not? It's the truth."

"Not compared with the girls at my new high school. Half of them look like models, and the other half *are* models," Molly said, only exaggerating a little.

Molly considered herself good-looking by Texas standards but here in California it was hard to feel pretty when surrounded by perfection. But what she wanted her mom to notice was that she was getting buff. All those late-night push-ups, all those early morning treks lugging her surfboard through the soft sand, and all the hours in the water and fighting to get past the breakers added up to the equivalent of a two-month free membership at the local gym.

"I wish I could stay and talk, but I've got to get to work. As it is, I'll probably have to stay late to get the grant finished."

Molly glanced at her mom lingering in the doorway and felt the slightest tinge of guilt. All her mom did anymore was work.

"Would you have left Dad if you knew it was going to be this hard?" she asked.

"I try not to think about that. I'd rather focus on the positive," Lynette said, fumbling for her car keys.

"And that would be . . . ," Molly wondered.

"You've got gunboats," Lynette said.

"I'm serious, Mom. Why did you leave him?"

"Look, I was in a bad situation, Molly. I didn't have a choice."

"You always have a choice. And I wish you would explain to me why you made yours," Molly said.

"I have to leave for work. You know how much trouble I get in if I'm late," Lynette said, avoiding the only real topic of conversation Molly wanted to have with her mother.

Lynette opened her arms for a hug good-bye, but Molly turned away from her. Still bothered by the memory of the woman's voice on the other end of her father's phone—Molly accepted long ago that she had not dialed the wrong number—she started to tell her mother about it now. But when Lynette cleared her throat with a sharp grunt—which is the sound she made prior to putting on her cheery face—Molly decided to keep her suspicions to herself. She, like her mother, was becoming a master at pushing her real feelings aside. But instead of putting on a cheery face, she put on her mantle of mad.

Even though she had promised to go to bed early, as soon as Lynette was ten minutes out of the door, Molly stepped into her jeans, slipped on a sweatshirt, grabbed her house keys and her cell, and left the trailer park, turning onto the avenue and heading for the Canary palm tree-lined piazza.

Molly hated to admit loving anything about Hermosa, but she did enjoy living in a town where you could leave your house at ten thirty at night, walk half a block, and be surrounded by a vibrant nightlife. In her old neighborhood in Lubbock, the streets rolled up at eight o'clock. But not here. At nine, it was just gearing up, and that was on the weekdays. Weekends, the action didn't pop until after ten. Her sleepy little beach town revved up after dark, populated by an odd mix of laid-back locals, moms and dads eating in restaurant patios while their kids played in the beachside promenade, and Hollywood hipsters down for the evening waiting in a line for admittance into black-couch clubs that pumped old-school Euro-techtronics onto crowded dance floors. As she neared Hermosa Avenue, she worked her way through a younger hip-hop tattoo and tank-top crowd that swarmed out of a funky pub and into the vinyl shop. Molly never ventured into the raucous bars with wall-to-wall clubbers or the well-heeled restaurants. She preferred to walk amidst the crowd, soaking up the atmosphere of the street, the music of the beach at night.

As Molly waited for the light at Hermosa Avenue to change, she was joined by four young women dressed in funky Western wear. One had on boots with a miniskirt. Another wore chaps with a bikini bottom and a Western shirt tied up just under her peekaboo lacy bra. Next to her was a bleached blonde dressed up like a Dallas Cowboy Cheerleader, and her other friend was wearing (and this is what really made Molly take notice) a black T-shirt with red lettering that said NOTHING QUITE LIKE A RAIDER GIRL. Molly supposed that the "Raider" in the tee could refer to the NFL football team, the Oakland Raiders, formerly the LA Raiders.

On the other hand, she could be a Red Raider girl. From Texas Tech. In Lubbock, Texas. Her dad's alma mater. And although Molly made it a rule to never actually talk to the people she saw on the street, she felt compelled to make an exception.

"Where y'all from?" she asked.

"West Covina," the Dallas Cowboy Cheerleader answered brightly.

Thank God they're not from Texas, Molly thought, and then asked out loud: "Where y'all goin' all dressed up like cowgirls? Halloween was a week ago."

The Dallas Cowboy Cheerleader explained that Wednesdays at Beanie's, one of the more notorious bars in the area, was Coyote Ugly night, where hot girls in Western wear were allowed to dance on the bar. "It's so awesome," she added.

"And it's a great way to meet people," the girl in the chaps chimed in.

Molly could only imagine the kind of people you would meet if you dressed like a stripper, bumped and grinded on top of the bar, and poured shots of tequila down a guy's throat.

"Plus, you get free beer," the Red Raider girl answered. "You should check it out. It's a blast."

"Thanks, anyway, but y'all have fun," Molly said. And as the light changed, the girls stepped out in the street on their way to what Molly was certain would be a supersize hangover.

Molly crossed the street and noticed a guy lying on the ground near the Wells Fargo ATM machine. He looked to be more than 250 pounds, at least. A foot patrol cop pulled his arms, and he lumbered to his feet. Molly had seen mean and dangerous drunks on a couple of occasions. She witnessed a wiry little man no bigger than Flea and totally out of control head-butt two cops who were trying to corral him into custody. She'd also seen a good-looking average Joe in a Hawaiian shirt arguing with a young blond woman over a bad call in a Steelers football game. He grabbed the girl's ponytail and yanked it so hard, Molly thought he might rip the hair right out of her scalp before a cop stepped in and broke it up. There were times when Molly thought that this particular entire city block was on a bender. Flea had warned her that fighting was so common at the piazza that it had been nicknamed "Thunderdome" after the classic *Mad Max* movie.

Despite the sometimes rowdy patrons, Molly was never scared or frightened while downtown. She'd never once been threatened. The only crime she had witnessed in the last two months of wandering the streets was intoxication. And she figured as long as she sidestepped the drunks and didn't get into conversations about football, she was relatively safe.

She walked past the piazza to the base of the pier where a bronze statue of lifeguard and famous surfer Tim

Kelly crouched on his board, riding down the face of a wave, looking out over the pier like a guardian angel. Kelly's death in the mid-sixties in a car accident had devastated the surfing world, especially the South Bay. In her two months at the beach, she had noticed that the younger surfers treated the fallen among them and the old-timers with enormous respect. And Kelly had been a member of the Jacobs Surf Team, one of the most famous in the history of the sport, along with many other surfing greats like Dewey Weber, Bing Copeland, and Greg Noll.

As Molly rounded the tile base of the statue, she saw another surfing legend, a more recent one. Duke sat at the foot of the statue, gazing out to sea, lost in thought. Not wanting to interrupt his reverie, she waited until he sensed her presence. He turned and looked at her, not at all surprised to see her at the pier near midnight.

"We have to stop meeting like this," Molly said, the third time she'd run into Duke at night in the last two and a half months.

Duke let loose a big guffaw. On various occasions, Molly had noticed a twinkle in his eye before, a glimmer of a smile on his lips, but this was the first time she had actually heard him laugh out loud.

"So have you been out partying with your buddies?" she asked.

"No, Archie and I grabbed a burger and a cup of coffee at Fat Face Fenner's. His wife had some kind of meeting, so he was free for a couple of hours," he said.

"Archie's married?" Molly asked.

"Yeah, and she keeps a leash on him shorter than the one on your surfboard. Which is one of the many reasons that, tonight, I am perfectly sober."

"Darn! I was hoping you'd been drinking," Molly said, only half teasing.

"That kind of attitude will not win you points with my AA group," Duke said.

Molly wondered if he really was a member of Alcoholics Anonymous or if he was teasing her back. She couldn't tell by the tone of his voice. But she decided not to press forward on a subject that serious. Keep it light—that was her motto.

"Well, the reason I hoped you'd been drinking is because I thought if you had, then maybe you would be inclined to tell me that story you owe me. Remember? The one about why you didn't kick me out that first day after you discovered I couldn't surf."

He looked at her and back out into the night. "Can you guess what my favorite book is?" he asked.

She considered the possibilities. It could be a book about surfing or with surfing in the title, but that seemed too easy. She considered a philosophical treatise, something with "Zen" in the title, like *Zen and the Art of Motorcycle Maintenance*, a paperback she had seen in her father's weird collection of books. She flirted with the idea of a book on politics. Maybe he was an Al Franken geek. In the end, she went with a classic.

"*The Old Man and the Sea*," she guessed, and for the second time tonight, he laughed out loud.

"Very close," he said, adding, "but the correct answer is *Gidget Goes Hawaiian*."

Although she was unfamiliar with the book, she was fascinated by its title. Who was Gidget, and why had she decided to go Hawaiian? Molly had to admit that it did not sound like the kind of book any guy, especially a guy named Duke, would claim as his all-time favorite.

"This sounds like a story I've got to hear."

Duke took the bait and began, "I was nineteen and stupid and in a bar in Long Beach drinking with two buddies who were younger and more stupid than I was. We were full of ourselves. We thought we wouldn't get caught because nobody knew us in Long Beach, which is what every stupid, drunk teenager thinks until the cops blow through the door. We got busted for disorderly conduct and underage drinking, and we made matters worse by trying to escape out the back door of the bar. So instead of getting off with a warning or a simple citation, they threw our asses in jail."

"I called my mom, but she was pissed as hell and decided that spending a couple of nights in the county jail would go a long way toward building my character. Well, it was awful. It was summer, and we were in the middle of a bitchin' heat wave. The jail was equipped with a steam heater that was stuck, so even though it was the middle of July, heat poured into the twenty-foot-square holding cell. There were fifteen bunks and thirty men. Most of them were drunk; a couple of them were crazy. I'm serious. They'd pace the corners of the cell and pound their fists against their skulls and moan. I don't know which was worse, the sounds or the smell, but I was convinced that I had landed in Dante's inferno along with the rest of the dregs of humanity.

"I panicked because I was afraid that by the end of the weekend I would cross over to the other side and become one of them, one of the moaners and groaners. Because we're all hanging on by a thread, and I knew that spending the weekend in that jail cell could stretch mine to the point of breaking. And that was when I saw it, peeking out from under one of the thin, gray mattress where it had been tucked away: a dog-eared copy of *Gidget Goes Hawaiian*. Don't ask me how a teenybopper novel about a pint-size surfer girl named Gidget got into the holding tank for drunks in Long Beach—it was weird karma—but I curled into a corner by myself and read that book cover to cover six times. It took me out of my hellish situation and into another world. I credit that book with keeping me alive."

He took a deep breath. "When I saw you walk up the sand holding that Malibu board, you looked the way I had imagined Gidget looked when she first hit the beach and took on the big boys of summer. And that's why I didn't kick you out of class."

He smiled and added nonchalantly, "Plus, you caught me on a good day."

That night after she got back home, she Googled Gidget and discovered that she was more than a character in a book; she was a real live surfing legend: Kathy "Gidget" Kohner. Her surf-borne exploits were detailed in the first *Gidget* book that her father wrote chronicling the summer the fifteen-year-old "girl-midget" hung out with a bunch of surf bums who lived in a shack in Malibu. Inspired, Molly browsed the web, surfing from one site to another, reading about other great woman surfers who broke past barriers to acceptance in the male-dominated sport: Queen Emma, Linda Benson, Joyce Hoffman, Mimi Munro, Margo Oberg, Rell Sunn, Jericho Poppler, Freida Zamba, and Lisa Andersen. All these women icons had one thing in common. For each and every one of them, surfing was less of a sport and more of a personal discovery. And she wondered if the reason surfers called road trips "safaris" was because surfing itself was a journey, not a destination.

Worn out, Molly's head hit the pillow at half past two and just before she closed her eyes, she thought she heard the soft roar of gentle waves lapping on the shore.

NINE

THE LATE NIGHT TOOK ITS TOLL AND THE NEXT MORNING, MOLLY OVERSLEPT UNTIL six. She was the last one to arrive to Surf Ed. Generally, the wind died down for a good hour right after sunup, but today a stiff breeze was blowing in clouds that clogged the clear sky. Molly didn't take the time to study the ocean, analyze the surf conditions, check for hazards on the board at the lifeguard tower, or even let Duke know she had arrived. She noticed her instructor and the other surfers were a couple hundred yards down the shore, going in at the Fourth Street tower. But she didn't want to waste water time trudging down the beach, not when a perfectly good break was firing right in front of her. Confident in her ability to handle it on her own, she plunged into the water away from the others. She dove under a wave as she had done countless times before on her way out to the surf zone, but when she surfaced and looked back over her shoulder, she saw that she was much farther out from the shore than she would have thought.

When she first entered the water, she had failed to notice a persistent band of churning, choppy, muddy water that contrasted with the aquamarine foam moving seaward. It extended from the shoreline through the surf zone and past the line of breaking waves. She dove under the next wave and when she came up, she realized she had been dragged into much deeper water and could no longer touch the bottom. Concerned that she might be pulled farther and farther from the shoreline, she decided to paddle her board back in. But as she managed to turn her board around, a wave broke over her head, grinding her into the sand.

There are times when a surfer has to decide whether "to hold or throw." Molly had been told that in most cases, it was smarter to hang on to the board, but she also knew that there were times when the only way to survive was to get rid of the board. She was knocked around by the undertow and her board whipped back and forth over her head, completely out of control. Afraid that at any minute it would knock her unconscious, she unstrapped the leash from her ankle and released it. She popped up, and the board flew past her, heading not back toward the shore as she had expected but out to sea. But without the board flip-flopping in her way, she was convinced that she could easily manage a swim back to shore.

Down the beach, Flea spotted his Texas friend. He alerted the others. "Looks like Molly's caught in the rip. I think she's in trouble."

Even though Molly punched her arms through the water powered by her newly acquired upper body strength, she was losing ground, as if she were trapped on a treadmill, unable to get off. She looked up in time to see another monster wave crash over her head. Pummeled by the choppy, disturbed water, she held her breath and clinched her eyes shut, tossed and turned by the devil wave. Finally, she popped her eyes open and with great relief saw what she thought was sky, only to discover seconds later that she was staring at the sandy bottom of the ocean floor at Eighth Street. The last few bubbles of air escaped, and she felt her lungs fill with water. For the first time in her life, she knew what it felt like to drown.

Unfortunately, Molly was not the only swimmer caught in the rip. On the beach, rescue operations were thrown into high gear. When Flea noticed Molly, the lifeguard on duty was already in the water, beating through the waves, going after two inexperienced out-of-towners who had been dragged out even farther than she had been. The lifeguard reached the first victim, who struggled against him. On the shore, Duke launched a paddleboard to assist the guard and signaled Kai to go in after their diva.

Molly pushed off the sand bottom with all her might and broke through to the surface, throwing up water from her lungs just before she was pounded by a third and even fiercer four-footer. She grabbed air before being dragged out even farther by the undertow. Panicked, she thrust her body out of the water, spewing out seawater. She waved her arms, frantically trying to get someone's attention onshore, to let Duke know she couldn't manage the situation, that she desperately needed help. But she was too late.

Because help was already there. Kai surfaced only a few feet away from her. "Grab hold," he said, extending his hand.

Choking back water and tears, she grasped his hand, and he pulled her to him and said, "I've got you. You're okay now. So just relax and enjoy the ride. This is better than anything at Disneyland."

"Are we having fun yet?" Molly wondered as she looked back to shore and watched the houses on the Strand fly past them at an alarming rate of speed.

Pulled a hundred feet down the shore in a matter of seconds, she clasped on to his arm like it was a life preserver, and he pulled her close to him with one arm and held on to his board with the other. He told her to relax and periodically reminded her to breathe.

"I thought I was going to die."

"That's why surfers call rip currents R-I-P. Because if

you don't know how to handle it, you can end up *resting in peace*. But there's a great lesson in the rip."

"I'm all ears," Molly said.

"You can't fight the water because it will always win. If you swim against the current, you will never get out of it. But if you ride it out, you will find your way to safer waters."

She leaned her head on his shoulder. In the strength of his embrace, she relaxed; her fear evaporated. Even though she was rocketing down the coastline in a channel of muddy water, she felt safe. And gradually, another stronger, different feeling took over, one that bubbled up from deep down inside somewhere unfamiliar. Riding the rip with Kai was as exhilarating as the first time she rode down the face of a wave. Part of it was that once she stopped struggling—when she gave herself up to the water—she could experience just how thrilling it was be pulled down the shoreline at seven miles per hour, which may not sound impressive by land standards, but on the water it felt faster than the speed of lightning. But the other part of it—and, if she was to be completely honest about it, the bigger part of it—was that she discovered that she liked the way it felt to be held in his arms. She liked it a lot.

She wondered if she was the first girl to ever fall in love in a riptide. Okay, to say that she had fallen in love was perhaps too strong a statement. But she had fallen into something more significant than just his arms. They surged up with the swell, and he pulled her to him a little tighter. She emitted an involuntary gasp of air, the same breathlessness that she had experienced the very first time she had seen him and she realized that her feelings for him had come full circle, back to the emotional beginning of their near-meeting.

"Well, thank you for saving my life and all. I really do appreciate it," she said.

He shrugged it off. The truth was, Kai was only too happy to go in after her. It was an opportunity, not an obligation. Because the rip might take him out to the place he wanted to be, much farther from shore, where some nice waves were firing.

They were washed four hundred more yards south before there was a break in the wave pattern and they finally emerged out of the surge of swiftly flowing water. Molly looked out to sea to Kai's destination. She watched the approaching swells, certain that the best set of the day was forming just over the horizon. When they were free of the current, she assured him that she could make it back to shore on her own.

Leaving him to follow his own pipe dream, she tumbled to shore on the crest of a three-footer. Only five minutes before, she had longed to touch solid ground. But as she trudged through the wet sand, she felt oddly sad to be leaving the water. She turned and shaded her eyes just in time to see Kai catch the best wave of the day, a spurt of perfection. Her breath quickened as she watched how beautifully he surfed the break, a lone surfer on a long, endless ride.

And she couldn't help but think to herself that falling in love was a lot like being in a rip: You don't know you're in it until it's too late.

Over the next few days, every time Molly saw Kai she was struck by a wave of feeling as topsy-turvy as the mad waters they rode together in the rip. And when they weren't together, she obsessed about him. She wondered if her dramatic change of heart was due to the fact that he had saved her life. She considered the possibility that she might be suffering from some kind of psychiatric disorder. She had read about the Stockholm syndrome in a political science class, named after a bank robbery incident in which bank robbers held bank employees hostage and the victims became emotionally attached to their kidnappers, even defending their captors after they were freed. It made sense to her that if a woman could convince herself she was in love with a man after he had threatened her life, a woman could certainly fall in love with a man after he saved it. Maybe Molly hadn't fallen in love in all; maybe she had fallen instead into some kind of pathology.

By the end of the week, she could not even engage Kai in the most casual of conversations without feeling her face blush. Instinctively, she knew if she couldn't get past this dangerous stage of intense attraction, she was destined to completely embarrass herself. Or worse. She knew from experience—the experience of others—that the best way to traverse the tricky waters of a new relationship was to talk it through with a girlfriend. She flipped open her cell, hoping Katie could help her make sense of her mixed-up feelings.

She hadn't talked to Katie since September. Keeping their friendship strong long distance had proven harder than either had first imagined. Theirs had been complicated further when Katie's parents confiscated her cell phone because of her prolonged talkfests with her boyfriend, whom they disliked as much as Molly did. Molly called her on her home line, but four sentences in, she heard a *click* and knew that one of Katie's parents was listening to their conversation. As if that weren't awkward enough, Katie was terse and noncommunicative, so Molly hung up after a brief exchange, convinced that whether or not they had been pushed apart or drifted apart, Katie could not be there for her now.

Frustrated, she opened her PowerBook, surfed the web, and found a Surviving Love—Self-help and Recovery chat room. Molly hesitated before logging in. She knew there were certain pitfalls in sharing your heart on the internet. One of the seniors at Garfield last year got *unaccepted* by his college of choice, a small Christian school in one of those Southern states that had a compass direction attached to the front of it like North Carolina or West Virginia, when the dean of admissions dropped in on his MySpace page and discovered he was gay.

Of course, an online chat room was not the same thing as a MySpace profile. The possibility of discovering like-minded souls with whom she could share her feelings was stronger than her reservations about expressing her very private point of view in a public forum. So, she took a deep breath and went for it; she logged in her user name, sexysax05, and posted her first comment: "Is it possible to fall in love without the other person falling in love back? Or does there have to be some kind of reciprocation to feel so incredibly connected?"

She was immediately barraged with criticism, but not concerning her comment. The problem was her screen name. She learned that it was hard to be taken seriously in a survivors' chat room with a screen name that began with "sexy." Four comments into the chat, Molly logged off, deciding that it might be more prudent to have conversations about your love life face-to-face with a real person. Even though the Internet offered a kind of anonymity, there was something more forgiving about words spoken aloud and drifting in the air instead of words written in the technological equivalent of stone—the hard drive. So instead of trying to find another chat room, Molly called Andrea and wheedled an invitation to come over and study.

"You know that old saying if a tree falls in a forest without anyone to hear it, does it make a sound? Well, this is what I want to know. If a girl falls in love but can't talk to anyone about it, do the feelings still exist?" Molly asked as she completed the next-to-last problem of her statistics homework. One benefit of being Andrea's friend was that Molly always accomplished a lot because Andrea insisted on multitasking.

Andrea looked up from her AP American history textbook incredulously. "What are you talking about, Molly?"

Molly popped up like a jack-in-the-box. "The problem is, I can't tell if Kai likes me. I mean, I know he likes me, but I don't know if he likes me in the way that counts. Because why would he? I've been a total bitch to him. And I keep wondering if he's changed or I've changed. I mean, maybe he's been the same but I couldn't see who he was because I was so angry. You know how it is when you just get mad about one thing and then everything annoys you? Really, if you look at it, the only reason he pissed me off is because he called me on my bullshit. Which is a good thing. Not a bad thing."

"God, Molly, you're so all about you tonight. Can't you see that I'm stressing?"

"Not any more than usual," Molly said honestly. Molly believed that Andrea overbooked her life. Anybody who had to schedule fun into fifteen-minute segments was headed for a breakdown. But she didn't tell Andrea that. Instead, she apologized and asked what Andrea's problem was.

"My birthday party is less than a month away and I was going to do this really cool eighties club theme at the Beach Club but my mother forgot to reserve it. She's such an idiot sometimes."

Molly had been to Andrea's house enough times to notice that her mother often began her cocktail hour in the middle of the afternoon; Molly wondered if booking the club had slipped her mind or if alcohol had clouded it.

"After I found out my mother screwed up, I called the chichi new boutique hotel in Manhattan Beach, but Cameron Diaz had already booked it. And I don't want to do it at a restaurant, because that is so yesterday."

"Why don't you have your party here? It's a beautiful house," Molly said.

"That's what my mom said too. She's totally okay with

moving all the furniture out of the second-floor living room, putting down a dance floor, and turning it into a disco if that's what I want. Do you think it would work? I mean, can you visualize it?"

At over 1,500 square feet, Andrea's second-floor living room was in fact bigger than some small nightclubs. Molly listened rapt as Andrea continued with a litany of elaborate party plans. Molly's own birthday parties had been held in her parents' backyard. But, of course, she didn't need so large a venue to accommodate her party list. No, all she needed was their picnic table under the patio awning. Her friends fit around a table of eight quite nicely, with plenty of elbow room.

"You're coming, of course," Andrea said.

Molly thought it strange that Andrea told her instead of asked her. What if Molly had other plans? But Molly dismissed the thought. If their relationship was not exactly on equal footing, it had made significant progress since their "special project" beginning.

"And go ahead and invite Kai, if you want to," Andrea said.

As thrilled as she was to be included on Andrea's guest list, Molly was equally as nervous about the prospect of inviting Kai. "I don't think I can. It feels too random."

"Have you ever asked a guy out before?"

"Yeah, last year I asked Dalton Reece out. But that was different."

"How so?"

"I didn't like him," Molly said, shrugging, deciding not to share that she had made out with this guy she did not like for almost two hours.

"If you didn't like him, then why did you ask him out?"

"Because he had a pulse and I was desperate for a date to homecoming."

Andrea formulated a social plan of attack for Molly while simultaneously creating a Revolutionary War History chart, a color-coded chronological spreadsheet detailing the events and the people of the times. Andrea was the undisputed master when it came to war charts. One of the other students in her AP class had offered to purchase a copy for five hundred dollars, but Andrea declined—not because she considered it cheating, but because she was unwilling to share information in a class where the teacher graded on the curve. Selling her study sheets would be like competing with herself.

"If you don't want it to sound like you're asking him out on a date, then ask the whole group: Kai, Riki, Ant, and Walter."

"You mean Flea and Waldo."

"Whatever. It's a big party, and a few others won't matter one way or the other."

Molly closed the book on her math problem and focused on the real problem at hand. "Don't you think it's a little weird for me to ask them to *your* party? Shouldn't you do that yourself?"

"I can't, because I don't know them," Andrea said, perturbed.

"My point exactly. No offense, but why would they want to come to a birthday party for a person they don't know?"

Exhausted by Molly's objections, Andrea finished highlighting a passage in yellow, indicating that it was an act of Congress and not George Washington, and looked up.

"Honestly, Molly, sometimes I think that you grew up in a cave. It doesn't matter if they know me or not. All you have to tell them is that you can get them into a party on the Strand where there will be live music and a keg. Those guys will be onboard, and I'm not talking surf, in a New York minute."

Now it was Molly's turn to be incredulous. "Your parents are actually going to let you have a keg at your party?"

"If you ask me one more question, Molly, we can no longer be friends."

It was the first time Andrea had used the word "friend" in reference to Molly, and the glorious sound of it erased any misgivings Molly had. So what if Andrea seemed unwilling to listen to Molly talk about Kai, even though in the weeks prior to Molly's falling in love in the rip he had been their main topic of conversation. The point was that here she was—Molly—in a beachfront mansion, with a girl on the A-list who had given her perfect opportunity to invite the guy she liked to an incredible party. Now that was what friendship was for.

TEN

"ASK ANY SURFER IN THE SOUTH BAY TO PICK THEIR FAVORITE SPOT OR WHERE THEY caught their last great wave and the chances are good they will answer El Porto," Waldo told Molly on a bright November morning as they rode in Kai's wagon to that venerable spot for Surf Ed.

A little up the coast north of Hermosa and a mile past the Manhattan Beach Pier, El Porto was a two-block-wide neighborhood that had once been a town in its own right. Surfers drove from all parts of Los Angeles to surf the famous beach break with lefts and rights that broke out over sandbars. Known as a northwest swell magnet, El Porto was home to bigger waves than in any other spot in the South Bay, especially during the winter months.

They arrived at the El Porto and parked in the beach lot, which was virtually empty, not a good sign. They unloaded their boards and started across the sand. Duke was already there, along with several other class members. Kai's group joined them and gazed past the shorebreak, searching for those epic, awesome waves. But the ocean was as flat as a lake.

"No wonder the parking lot's empty," Kai added.

It was low tide and the waves were breaking inside, almost on the shore. The legendary waves of El Porto had traveled south. Today, it was hardly worth the trouble to put a board in the water. Flea suggested that they walk down the jagged rock jetty and jump off into deeper waters where they could free-dive into the surrounding kelp beds. AJ, always prepared, pulled out a snorkel and fins from his surf bag.

Molly followed the others as they climbed the slippery rocks to the end of the jetty where the small waves were even more tempered by the rocks. One by one the surfers jumped into the rolling, surge-swept kelp forest. Molly dove in and pushed her way through a canopy of golden brown kelp. The leaflike blades, floating brown mats, gently slapped against her body. Feeling peaceful and calm, Molly flipped over and floated on her back, drifting away from the others. She closed her eyes and let the gentle rays from the early morning sun warm her face. She could occasionally feel one of the tentacles of the kelp forest rise up to tickle her behind her knees.

And then she heard it. A high-pitched chirping sound, like nothing she had ever heard before. She opened her eyes and heard a response, this one more like rattling or clicking. Flea swam to her, excited. "It's dolphins. They're very close."

Flea and Molly were soon joined by the others; all of them had heard the dolphins singing. Kai pointed to a spot thirty yards away, where the first of several flying fish skidded across the water. The disturbed water could indicate that dolphins were feeding in their midst.

"Cue the dolphins," AJ exclaimed at the first explosion of water droplets.

Seconds later, and as announced, six dolphins blew out of the water, arched over, and dove back under in one synchronized movement. The surfers took off, swimming as fast as they could in the direction where they had spotted the sleek marine mammals. To see dolphins in the South Bay waters was not uncommon, but to actually swim with them was trickier because they were much faster than humans. The only chance a surfer had of actually catching up to them was if the dolphin slowed down and allowed it to happen. As Molly raised her head and took an excited breath, she saw two of the dolphins surface together, one smaller than the other, suggesting perhaps mother and child. They had changed direction from the original sighting, probably following the school of fish. Molly yelled at the others, reporting that the pod was now headed more south than west. The swimmers treaded water and eagerly scanned the swells, waiting for the pod to reappear.

But instead of dolphins, the head of a large, sleek sea lion broke the surface of the water, barking ferociously.

All her surfing buddies immediately turned tail and started swimming in the opposite direction, heading back to shore, the pursuit of the dolphins quickly abandoned.

"Where are you going? It's just a sea lion," Molly yelled after them, thinking to herself that no matter how hard she tried, she would never be able to understand people from California. Apparently, they weren't afraid to swim with the sharks, but they were terrified of one little sea lion. The sea lion ducked back under the water, and so did Molly. She had seen sea lions from a distance, rocking back and forth on the marine buoy at the entrance of King Harbor, but she had no idea how large they were until this one careened toward her like a three-hundred pound cannonball and then darted off again as if to engage her in some kind of underwater conversation.

"Get out of the water!" Flea screamed, swimming back for Molly.

But Molly wanted to stay and swim with the sea lion. She had the most amazing feeling that this animal was trying to communicate with her.

"Don't get all SeaWorld on me. That's not a dolphin. That's a junkyard dog, except that sea lions have a bite that is ten times stronger than a canine's. Oh, and did I mention, a mouth full of bacteria," Flea said.

Flea turned toward the shore and caught the first wave in. Molly missed that one and waited for the next. She crested the wave and stroked toward the shore, her face in the water.

Stunned, she watched as the sea lion swam right beneath her, turning belly up and looking at her with sad, soulful eyes. The two were so near each other in their underwater dance that Molly could almost reach out and touch her spiky whiskers. But up close, Molly could also see that something was terribly wrong. And she was frightened. Not for herself. But for this magnificent animal. The sea lion's neck was encircled by the remnants of gill net that had ripped through its skin, creating a gaping wound all along her throat. There was blood in the water.

And just like that, she was gone.

Molly swam back to shore as fast as she could and trudged through the white water, tears streaming down her face. At first Duke was concerned that she had been bitten. Although he knew that there hadn't been more than ten sea lion attacks on humans on the West Coast in the last century, he also knew if you got close enough to one of them, invading their territory or their food source, they would bite. And what had been even more disturbing was that in recent years, they had seen more and more troubled marine animals washed up onshore, disoriented and suffering from domoic acid poisoning, a toxic algae bloom that damages a mammal's central nervous system. Wild animals could not be trusted, and sick or wounded animals even less so.

"She's hurt really bad," Molly said. She described what she had seen, and Duke surmised that the sea lion had gotten caught up in the monofilament used by gillnet fisheries.

Duke flipped out his cell and called his old surfing buddy, Archie, who had saved dolphins, whales, seals, and even seabirds, but most of his work with the sea mammal rescue organization involved those junkyard dogs of the ocean: sea lions.

"A gill-netted sea lion has a very limited amount of time to live because the wound almost always becomes septic," Duke said matter-of-factly.

"We have to find her before that happens," Molly said.

For the next few days, Molly quit obsessing about Kai and instead obsessed about the sea lion. She anxiously checked her cell for messages from Duke in between every single class the rest of the week, thinking there had been a sighting of the wounded animal. After school, she hiked down to El Porto thinking that the sea lion might resurface in the rocks where they had first seen her.

"If you keep investing all this emotional energy into an animal you only met once, you're going to have to name it," Flea said, trying to tease her out of her funk.

Molly shook her head. If she was to give it a name, she would have to admit how personally involved she was with its fate. There were hundreds, if not thousands, of sea mammals injured by nets and toxins poured into the ocean. Why not stress over them? Why had she poured so much time and emotion and energy into that one? At least she could refer to it as "that sea lion." If she was to name it, she would have to call it "my sea lion."

But that sea lion had swum beneath Molly and had turned its belly to her the way a dog does in an offer of submission. She would never forget those deep brown eyes. Nor could she erase the memory of the seared skin; the ugly, open gash. Alone at El Porto at sunset, Molly watched the last rays of light dance across the sparkling waters. It had been three days since Molly first saw that sea lion. Who the hell was she kidding? It was not *that* sea lion; it was *her* sea lion, whether she gave it a name or not.

And for Molly's sea lion, time was running out.

• • •

When Molly thought she couldn't bear it any longer, she walked home. Duke came by just as she was entering the park.

"The guard at Thirty-third Street spotted your sea lion on the jetty. Archie's meeting me there with the harbor patrol," Duke said, climbing into his beat-up red truck. Molly quickly jumped into the passenger's side.

As Duke turned north onto the coast highway, Molly considered that at the exact same moment she had been standing on the shore soaking up the sunset, her sea lion might have been lurking nearby on the other side of the jetty or in the kelp beds close to shore. Molly wondered if the sea lion had caught sight of her on the beach. Did animals in the wild recognize different humans the way domesticated ones did? Was the sea lion looking for Molly? Could she have sensed that Molly was looking for her?

"Your sea lion's in trouble, Molly. I don't know if we can save her," Archie said as he led Duke and Molly across the jagged rocks of the jetty to the spot where she had tumbled after a failed rescue attempt with a net and fallen into a crevasse, twenty feet down.

Molly hunched over the rocks and saw that her sea lion was wedged into the crevasse at the bottom of the jetty; the water surged over her head in steady intervals.

Trapped, she struggled to raise her nose and push her forehead out of the water in an attempt to gasp for air. The tide was rising, and very soon the sea lion would be totally emerged in water.

"We have to do something. We can't let her drown," Molly insisted.

"There are times when there's nothing you can do to save an animal. Sometimes, you have to let them go," Duke said, preparing Molly for the worst.

"Okay, but this is not one of those times," Molly said.

"You stay here, Molly, and keep an eye on her," Archie told Molly. "We'll see what we can do."

Leaving the net on the rocks beside Molly, Archie and Duke climbed off the jetty to prepare for a water approach. Molly watched helplessly as the water from the surge covered the sea lion again and again and again. Even in the darkness, she could see the desperate, hopeless look on the sea lion's face as she gasped for short breaths of air in between the waves that relentlessly and mercilessly covered her in water. Molly considered for a moment that Duke might be right: that they wouldn't be able to save her, that the sea lion would drown in a watery grave trapped in the rocks in the jetty. And she wondered that if everything did have its purpose—like her mother always said—then maybe her purpose in moving from Texas to California was to be with this animal during her last minutes of life.

While the sea lion struggled for breath, Archie borrowed an orange cone floatation device from the lifeguard. He fastened it around Duke's waist and then tethered it to himself with a rope line.

Archie struggled to keep the tension on the line taut so that the pounding surf wouldn't crash Duke onto the rocks as he waded through the tumultuous white water. From her vantage point above, Molly guided Duke to the spot where the sea lion was wedged. Duke grabbed on to one of the craggy stones and leaned forward. His face was only inches away from the sea lion; he stuck his hand below the surface trying to find what was obstructing her release, but he couldn't find anything from that position.

Duke dove under the water to get a better look. Molly worried that in the murky night waters he wouldn't be able to see anything at all. Duke popped up, excited; his voice tinged with hope as he yelled, "The netting's trapped on the rock."

He pulled out a pocketknife from the pocket in his board shorts and dove under the water again, cutting the netting free. With a huge roar, the sea lion emerged from her watery tomb and back onto the rocks, only a few feet from Molly.

Even in the dark, Molly could see that she was much

thinner than she had been just days before. Her bark was weak and raspy. Afraid that if she waited for the men she might lose the opportunity altogether, Molly grabbed the net Archie left behind and cautiously approached the sea lion, creeping up behind the animal over the wet, slippery rocks. Molly inched forward to a couple of feet away from the animal and then froze.

This was it. The one chance. Either she would bag her, or she would lose her. And if she lost her, it would probably be forever.

Molly quickly tossed the hoop in front of the sea lion. Startled, the sea lion lurched forward and landed right into the net, jerking Molly forward with the force of her weight. Molly lost her footing, slipped, and fell, cutting her knee on the jagged rocks. And as blood gushed from her leg, she screamed at her sea lion, who struggled against the netting, "Don't fight me or we'll both die!"

Even as she said it, she knew it was ridiculous to attempt negotiations with a wild animal.

Or not.

Amazingly, her sea lion stopped, only for a few seconds, but long enough for Archie and Duke to reach them. Archie took control of the net, and Duke radioed the harbor patrol, who was idling just off the shore. The captain flashed on the searchlights and pulled up beside the breakwater near the netted sea lion. Together, the three of them heaved her onboard, and she landed in a heap at the stern of the boat.

Molly flew down the dock at King Harbor just in time to see Archie and the two men from the boat hoist the sea lion from the boat into a cage. Up close, Molly could see that the cut around her neck was deeper, more inflamed, a veritable necklace of pain. At first, the sea lion was agitated, but she calmed down once the cage was settled in the back of Archie's truck, where it was to ride to the Marine Mammal Care Center in San Pedro.

Archie told Molly that only about half of the sea mammals he rescued survived. "But she's not in as bad shape as I thought she'd be. She's got a chance," Archie said, explaining that the mammal would be treated and then rereleased into the ocean.

Molly asked if she might be able to visit the sea lion, to check on her progress, but Archie explained the center did not encourage human contact; they never treated the animals they rescued like they were pets. Their mission was to heal the wounded animals, rehabilitate them if necessary, and return them to the ocean as wild as they were when they'd rescued them. Molly nodded, accepting that she would never make the trip to San

Pedro to visit the sea mammal while she was recovering.

She gazed into the cage and silently said her good-byes to her sea lion. In that dimly lit, empty parking lot, with the slosh of the breakwater a sweet, distant murmur, she realized that the sea lion had never been hers, not even in that moment when they danced together in their underwater ballet. If anything, it was the other way around.

She had belonged to it.

Grateful to Duke for having given her the opportunity to say her good-byes, Molly walked across the parking lot to his waiting truck. On the back bumper she noticed a sticker that read, EDDIE WOULD GO. Intrigued, Molly asked Duke on the ride home what the bumper sticker meant. "Who is Eddie, and where would he go?"

Duke laughed and answered, "Anywhere he wanted. Eddie Aikau was a surfing legend and all-around waterman who knew no limits. The master of big Hawaiian surf in the seventies. His last ride was in a double-hulled canoe on a journey to retrace the ancient Polynesian passage between Hawaii and Polynesia. Right away, they got into trouble. Their canoe capsized in the rough Molokai channel. The crew hung on all night, but by morning help hadn't come and they were being smashed by the trade winds. Eddie volunteered to swim to Lanai to get help and took off. That night, the rest of the crew was rescued after an airline pilot spotted their flare. But Eddie was never seen again," Duke said as they drove down Valley Drive.

"Do any of your stories have a happy ending?" Molly wondered.

"Eddie lived and died doing what he loved best. What's sad about that? His last words to the crew were, 'Don't worry. I can do this,'" Duke said.

"So his last words turned out to be a lie?" Molly asked.

"More like a miscalculation," Duke corrected her. "The point is, life seldom turns out the way you expect it to. So you might as well enjoy the ride."

ELEVEN

"GEE, BRAIN, WHAT ARE WE GOING TO DO TONIGHT?" FLEA ASKED BUZZ BEFORE SCHOOL on the last day before their Thanksgiving break, referring to *Pinky and the Brain*, a totally weird cartoon series that had become a cult favorite among the guys at Beach High who liked to surf the web as much as they did the waves.

"Same thing we do every night, Pinky," Buzz shot back the pat response. "Try to take over the world."

Flea had recently acquired the complete collection of *Pinky and the Brain*. He and Buzz had watched the entire three-year series twice already and had memorized enough of the episodes to drive Kai crazy; he was not a fan. The three guys and Waldo walked in a pack down the open-air corridor before their second-period class.

Just arriving at school and looking disheveled as usual, Molly ran to catch up with them. As they approached their lockers, Kai suggested that since tomorrow was the beginning of Thanksgiving break and there was no school, "We should do something tonight."

Molly perked up with interest. Was she included in the *we*?

"Are you pondering what I'm pondering, Pinky?" Flea asked, conjuring up his best imitation of the mad scientist.

"Um, I think so, Brain, but where will we get rubber pants our size?" Buzz responded in character.

"You guys spend way too much time in front of your computer," Kai said.

"Says the man who sold his EverQuest character for four hundred dollars. How much time did you spend on that?" Flea said, reminding Kai of his own addiction.

"That was last year, and I got over it," Kai said.

Kai had been a major fan of role-playing video games, but his passion for electronically manipulated fantasy worlds had subsided in the last year, replaced by an interest in the real one. His skill as a waterman had given him cachet into the fraternity of surfers, which in turn had given him entrance into all the bars and cafés along the piazza.

"Let's hang out downtown and maybe grab a burger at the Lighthouse Café."

The Lighthouse was a beachfront jazz bistro, a Hermosa Beach icon that resisted change. Its proximity to the water had made it a favorite among surfers; it had been a Los Angeles legend since before Kai was even born.

"Sounds good, brah," Waldo explained, "but I committed to some serious alone-time with Riki."

Buzz, too, was a "no-can-do"; his parents had signed him up for an SAT tutor. Kai turned to Flea and Molly. "You guys wanna come? Judi Jansen's singing tonight. She's really hot."

"Sure," Molly said, swallowing her excitement.

Flea shrugged apologetically. "Sorry, dude and dudette, but I have to go to my sister's Bat Mitzvah. And I can't miss it, because she hates me already."

"That's so cool. I didn't know you were Jewish," Molly said.

Flea smiled and shrugged. "Only on major holidays."

"Sounds like it's just you and me," Kai said to Molly, who frankly was more than okay with the way "you and me" sounded.

"Hey, I got tonight off," Lynette told Molly when she came out of her bedroom after waking up at six in the evening. "I thought maybe we could go out to dinner and catch a movie. Maybe even go shopping. It's been a long time since we've done that."

"I can't, Mom. I've already got plans. I'm going out with a friend."

"A girlfriend or a guy friend?" Lynette asked.

"A guy friend, but please do not make this into a big deal," Molly answered.

Ignoring her daughter's request, Lynette perked up, suddenly interested. "Do you have a date? When do I get to meet him?"

"You don't because I'm meeting him downtown. And it's not a date. We're just friends. Please don't ask me any more questions, okay?"

"Is he a nice boy?"

"Mom, I really don't want to talk about it. So, I'll see you later. And don't worry. I promise to be back before Sunday."

"And I'll be home waiting up for you when you get back. So see you at midnight."

"Back by two at the latest," Molly said, opening the door.

"Be home by one," her mother said as Molly closed the door, negotiations completed.

A light fog tiptoed in off the water as Molly crested the hill and glimpsed the heart of downtown. She zipped up her sweatshirt jacket as she wandered through the mist to the foot of the pier. Molly had passed by the Lighthouse dozens of times before on her late-night sojourns, but she had never ventured inside.

Kai was waiting for her in front of the club, leaning

against the railing, his demeanor suggesting a casual easiness with his surroundings that in all her midnight excursions she had yet to muster. But he was born to the scene that she was still in the process of discovering. They had over an hour before Judi took the stage, so Kai suggested that they sit on the patio and order some food and drinks before going inside the club. Outside space heaters kept the evening chill at bay, and Molly didn't mind the light fog. The most positive thing about not having a hairdo per se was that a little moisture in the air never ruined a messy bun. As she and Kai elbowed their way to an empty table, she noticed that the patrons were mostly in their mid-twenties, some older, a few younger. But they all seemed to know Kai. People nodded and waved, and a couple of other surfers actually called him by name.

They settled on a small, high table near the door. Molly climbed on the bar stool, a little uncertain. Sitting in a chair where her feet couldn't touch the ground made her feel at a distinct disadvantage. A young waitress wearing black pants and a white starched shirt sashayed over to take their order, batting her eyelashes. Molly noticed a diamond stud on her brow.

"So what would you like to drink?" the waitress asked.

Good question. Molly wondered if Kai would order a beer. And if he did, would he expect her to? And did he have a fake ID? Would he even need one? And if he had one, would he expect her to have one too? Molly wasn't opposed to drinking. In fact, it was on her to-do list, right up there with having sex. But she hadn't planned on doing it in the fall of her junior year. The waitress shifted impatiently, waiting for Molly.

"You go first. I'm still deciding," Molly said finally.

"I'll have a Coke," Kai said.

"Make that two," Molly said a little too quickly. The relief in her voice was palpable.

Kai looked at her quizzically. "What? Did you think I'd try to order a beer or something?"

"I thought you might. Everybody seems to know you here."

"Which is exactly why I wouldn't," Kai said.

Molly smiled, relieved. As she surveyed the crowd, she noticed a growing contingency of local surfers that, for some reason, struck her as odd. And she wondered aloud to Kai why so many young surfers were drawn to a club that was known for jazz.

"How do you know who's a surfer and who's not? 'Cause we don't all wear Hawaiian shirts, you know."

"Right. Only to weddings and funerals," Molly said.

"You catch on fast," he said.

Molly pointed at two guys in the corner, both exceedingly

tan and one sporting visible tattoos. "That's the real deal," she said.

Testing her, Kai pointed to another guy at the other end of the patio with a drop-dead-gorgeous date. He was also exceedingly tan and buff, but unlike the first guy, he sported four piercings on his brow and two on his lips. "What about that guy?" he asked.

"Doubtful," she said.

"Why?" he asked.

"Because surfers like tattoos, but they seldom go for piercings—except for ears, which are totally optional," she said confidently.

"Damn. You are good."

Kai shared his own opinion on the Hermosa relationship between jazz and surfers. He said although some said it was a kind of New Age, spiritual connection, he was convinced that it had to do with the bar's proximity to the sand. It was one of the first places off the beach where you could get a beer and a burger and park your board out front, which held a huge attraction because they were only a heartbeat away from the next awesome set. Kai said that you could spot the really hardcore surfers as they lined up at the bar simply by the way they held their heads with an ear cocked toward the ocean. Like a dog smelling the breeze, they sipped their beer and listened for some sign, a murmur of wind or a slap of a wave. Good surf spoke in low whispers before the firing break roared.

While Molly and Kai talked on the patio, more and more people drifted in from the plaza. By the time they heard the first stirrings of instruments tuning up, a large crowd had managed to sandwich itself inside. Kai held Molly's hand so they wouldn't get separated as they left their table, squeezed through the crowd, and made their way through the long, dimly lit club. On either side of the stage were a scattering of tables, all full; it was standing room only. The walls above the bar that stretched the back of the room were dotted with old photographs of jazz legends who had played there throughout the bar's long history. In the corner were a green-lit clock and a couple of red glowing ship lanterns that cast a warm glow on the stage.

The jazz quartet opened with an instrumental number. Consisting of a drummer, pianist, bassist, and saxophonist, they were a solid ensemble, blending seamlessly together in a rhythmic question-and-answer session that gave the drummer a chance to show off his skills. Kai explained that he had first come to see Judi's act because of the drummer. Kai played the snare drums in jazz band at school and although he readily admitted that he himself was not all that talented, he knew enough to appreciate greatness in others. As the other musicians jammed through the coda,

Kai leaned in and whispered in Molly's ear: "I'm really glad you could come tonight. I really wanted you to hear Judi sing. Because she reminds me of you."

He slipped his arm around her waist, and in that simple touch, Molly experienced at full throttle the one emotion she had resolved herself to not have this evening and that was hope. She had to stifle herself from bursting into some kind of celebratory love song before the real jazz singer took the stage. And while Molly was luxuriating in the possibility that whatever that thing was that had happened to her in the rip had perhaps happened to him as well, a small, wiry woman of a certain age, lots older than Molly's mom, brushed past her. Her hair was a wild mass of curls, pulled off her face with a series of rhinestone-studded barrettes. She had a tiny scar on her left cheek from a botched chemical peel, and a throbbing vein on her forearm. She smelled like the sixties (or the way Molly imagined the sixties must have smelled, a heavy, musky odor). The crowd parted for her as she snaked her way to the stage.

"That's Judi Jansen," Kai said.

Molly studied the jazz singer as she climbed the stairs to the stage, searching for similarities. She had to admit that they were about the same size. In fact, Judi had an amazing body, small, compact, and bristling with energy. Molly conceded that this woman was very interesting looking and she was flattered by that particular fact, but that did not erase the most obvious one: Judi Jansen was OLD.

"Why do I remind you of her? Is it because we're both short?"

He shook his head.

"Well, it can't be the way I sing. Because I can't carry a tune in a bucket."

"It goes deeper than that. Just listen and you'll see."

Judi took the stage to a round of anticipatory applause. As the musicians jammed through a long musical introduction, the room rustled with the sounds of settling in. Drinks were ordered; patrons shifted in their chairs. People who were standing found the best view. Judi grabbed the mic and looked into the crowd with a piercing gaze that demanded their attention. A comfortable silence descended upon the crowd.

"I wish I may, I wish I might, have that one wish I wish tonight," she sang.

It was an upbeat original tune written by a local Hermosa Beach artist—smooth jazz—and Judi sang it straight, with no unnecessary scatting or trilling. Her voice was strikingly clear, but at times took on a smoky quality. And Molly noted with a sense of irony that the lyrics were all about hope, the one emotion Molly had promised herself to avoid tonight at all costs.

The room was packed to overflowing. Even so, more wandered through the door from the street, lulled into the venerable bar by Judi's melodious crooning. Standing next to Molly, a twenty-eight-year-old in a sleeveless shirt, revealing neck-to-wrist tattoos and sporting an Aussie leather outback hat, nodded to the soft beat of the snare.

The singer crooned, "Upon that rising star I'm scheming; To touch the prince of whom I'm dreaming."

The young man next to Molly tipped his hat in Judi's direction and smiled, more than a little bit smitten, like someone who had fallen in love for the first time. And he was not alone. All over the bar, young men watched, spellbound. Their loud, brazen, beer-fed conversation muffled to a whisper.

"I've tossed all reason to the side. You cannot duck, you cannot hide. My wish is strong, so play along, you cannot fight. That wish will make you mine tonight," Judi sang.

Molly wondered how this middle-aged jazz singer could make ultracool surfer types thirty years her junior take a break from their beers and guac to hang on to her every note. Even Kai seemed momentarily stilled by her temptress spell. He pulled Molly closer and whispered in her ear, "See what I mean?"

Not really. But she was working real hard to try to understand. But three hours and two sets later, she still failed to see the connection between herself and Judi.

The last note of the final set still lingering in the air, they left the Lighthouse and stepped out in the night. It was just after one o'clock, and the piazza bristled with life. The patios outside the bars and café were still buzzing with diehard partyers who seemed in no hurry to let the evening go.

As they walked through downtown, Molly and Kai discussed the effect Judi seemed to have on men, especially younger ones. Kai, who had ceased to be freaked out by the effect her singing had on him, summed it up succinctly: "She's hot."

"And I remind you of her?" Molly said, amazed.

"Yeah. Totally."

"And you know I don't sing? We've established that, right?" Molly asked.

"You can't carry a tune in the proverbial bucket," Kai confirmed.

Molly stopped, tilted her chin, lowered her lashes, and looked Kai straight in the eye. "So are you saying that I'm hot?"

"No, that's not what I meant," Kai answered honestly, and then added, trying to make amends, "Molly, you're really cute."

"Cute" was a word that should be used to describe puppies or perky little tube tops or purple daisies on flip-flops. And cute certainly would never be used to describe the woman she had seen performing onstage.

Some people lived in a perpetual state of hope, but Molly was not one of them. Hope, for her, was the brass ring on the carousel, hung out on a metal arm for riders to grab to get the grand prize. All night long that brass ring of hope had appeared to be within her reach. But each time she flew by and felt it within her grasp, it was yanked away from her, just inches out of reach.

"The reason you remind me of Judi is because I think you're going to get better and better the older you get. I mean, you're good now, really, really good. But you're going to be amazing when you're old," Kai said, explaining.

"What?" Molly said, completely caught off guard by the weirdest compliment she had ever received.

"Duke says that people are like red wines; they peak at different times. Some are drinkable at ten years, but others never reach their full potential until fifty," Kai said.

"Exactly how old do you think I'll be when I reach this state of amazingness?"

"Probably about forty."

"Okay, I was feeling a little down today, but you just moved me into the neighborhood of totally depressed."

"Then why do you look like you're about to smile?"

The twitch in the corner of Molly's mouth upturned

into a grin. He took her hand, and they walked across the piazza, the mica in the pavement shimmering like glitter. When they passed Java Boy, Molly turned to him. Emboldened by his move, she made a bold move of her own. "This is where we almost first met," Molly said.

"It is? Are you sure?" Kai asked. Now it was his turn to be confused.

Molly explained the circumstances of that near-miss first meeting, how she had been literally run down by the marauding skateboarder. "There I was all sprawled out on the pavement, feeling dumber than a box of hair. It was like the whole world was laughing at me. And then you spoke up."

"That was you?" Kai asked, remembering the incident but having never seen the victim's face.

"The one thing I regretted was that I never did say thank you for demanding an apology from that bitch."

"I don't think I deserve thanks, because the woman never did say she was sorry."

"Yeah, but the point is that what you *did* say made me feel better. So, thank you."

Kai smiled, pleased, and offered to give her a ride home, but she declined, saying that she'd rather walk, not caring whether she made her negotiated curfew or not. The truth was, the thought of being totally alone with him in a car was way too much to deal. She didn't think she could live through the eight minutes it would take to fight their way out of the parking lot and through the end-of-night traffic until they reached the quiet trailer park on top of the hill. Eight achingly long minutes that would drag on and on in anticipation of the one monumental moment that would follow. She couldn't face the prospect of a good night kiss or, worse yet, the absence of one. No, it was better to say their good-byes on the piazza in a very public place. She had flirted with hope too many times that night to face disappointment again. She thanked him once again and started out for home.

"Molly . . ."

She turned back around, facing him.

"You're welcome," he said as he reached out, grabbed her hand, and gently pulled her to him.

There on the piazza, in front of hundreds of people, he kissed her. Molly assumed that all first kisses were somewhat awkward; that had certainly been her experience up until now. But when Kai leaned in, she didn't worry about where she should put her arms or if she should purse her lips or leave them slightly open. He tasted exactly the way she'd imagined he would, slightly salty. She had read about kisses that "leave you breathless"; this was not that kind of kiss. In fact, it was just the opposite. Kissing Kai felt as natural as breathing. Only better. Way better.

• • •

When she tiptoed into the trailer, she found her mother sound asleep on the sofa in front of the TV, which was blaring out a rerun of *Friends*, the episode where Rachel discovered she was pregnant. Molly whispered that she had arrived home safe and amazingly close to curfew, secretly hoping her mother wouldn't wake up and start in with a million nagging questions. Luckily, Lynette mumbled good night and sank back into the cushions. Relieved that she wasn't forced into a prolonged conversation that might shatter her dreamy mood, Molly gratefully escaped to her room alone, the spell of that first kiss unbroken.

She closed her door, stripped off her clothes, and riffled through her T-shirt drawer for something appropriate to sleep in on the night Kai first kissed her. She settled on a concert T-shirt from *White Trash with Money*, figuring that if she had been kissed by Kai, she might as well go for the gold and sleep with Toby Keith.

She slid into the oversize T-shirt, crawled into bed, and snuggled into the covers. She licked her bottom lip in hopes (yes, once again) that the taste of Kai would have lingered. But it was gone, as fleeting as the kiss itself. Before she closed her eyes, she turned over and looked out the narrow window above her bed. The fog had completely blanketed the sky; there was not a single star in the heavens. She felt hope, once again, slipping away. And then, suddenly, a patch of midnight opened up and she thought she saw a distant light, a celestial body to wish upon, and a good omen to cap off the evening. She let the words of Judi's song replay in her head.

"So I advise you, open both your eyes and see the light. That star will make you mine tonight."

Oh, so satisfied, Molly rolled over on top of Toby Keith (the T-shirt, that is) and fell into a deep, deep sleep.

TWELVE

A KISS IS JUST THAT. A KISS. IT DOESN'T MEAN ANYTHING. IT DOESN'T GUARANTEE anything. Just because a guy kisses you doesn't mean that he's going to call you. Or IM you. Or put you on his top eight on MySpace. Or even drop by and say hi. Which, incidentally, if we're keeping track, and Lord knows I'm not, but if we were keeping count—the guy in question, the one who kissed me, hasn't done any of the above. But that doesn't make the kiss in question any less wonderful. But, you have to remember, no matter how wonderful a kiss seems at the time, wonderfulness does not imbue it with meaning. A kiss, no matter how spectacular, has no residual meaning other than what it meant at the fleeting moment in time at which it was delivered. Because a kiss is just that—a kiss. Lips meet. Lips part. Tongues tease. And then it's over, right? Or am I missing something here?

Molly read her blog entry seven times before dragging it to the trash bin. Purged by the act of writing, she had no further desire to digitally share her innermost thoughts. After the experience with Kai in the rip, Molly had been desperate to discuss the depth and range of her emotions. But after their first quote-unquote kiss, she felt just the opposite. She dodged her mother's questions, ignored an e-mail from Katie asking if she had met anybody yet. And she avoided Andrea, who left a dozen messages on her cell, pestering her with questions about Kai and whether or not he was coming to her party the following Saturday.

Interestingly, Molly and Kai spent the week after Thanksgiving break successfully avoiding each other. Neither of them made any attempt to find any "serious alone-time," as Waldo would call it. Plus, both days of Surf Ed. were thrown off kilter because Duke was absent, home sick. Archie filled in as substitute. The kids liked Archie well enough, but the problem was that Archie was a quintessential lifeguard and he never missed an opportunity to teach what he called "preventative lifeguarding skills." As a result, the kids spent far more time on the sand than in the water. He gave lectures on first aid, CPR, ocean safety, rescue techniques. It was a review for most of the Dawn Patrol because they had completed four grueling years of junior guards. Bored from the beginning, AJ said the lectures were a "total snooze," and Waldo concurred, bragging that he could do

CPR in his sleep. But Molly, who had missed those summer programs where grommets were whipped into seaworthy shape by the senior lifeguards, paid close attention. Having gained a healthy respect for wind and water, she thought it prudent to learn everything she could since, so far, it seemed that she'd had to rescue her own self at regular intervals.

But on the Thursday session, even Molly complained when Archie assigned Waldo to be her victim for a paddle-board rescue.

"Oh, come on, can't I start with Flea and work my way up to someone bigger?" Molly asked, certain that her size would be a disadvantage. How could she save someone a foot taller and fifty pounds heavier than she was?

But Archie taught her several techniques for rescuing people larger than herself. The entire session was spent practicing mock rescues using lifeguard cones and paddle-boards. After Molly successfully rescued Waldo a total of five times (once she pretended to let him drown just on general principle), she decided to test Andrea's theory and see exactly where she stood with the group and with Kai. As they packed away their boards, Molly casually mentioned that she had a connection to a party on the Strand where there would be beer and live music. Waldo said yes as soon as the word "party" left her mouth. AJ jumped in with a definite "I'm in" at the mention of beer. Riki perked up at the mention of "live music" because Riki was an amazing dancer and welcomed any opportunity to show off her skills. Buzz agreed, even though he was convinced the party would blow. And Flea said if he'd go if Molly was going.

"We'll see," Kai said. "I'm not really all that into parties."

Molly's heart sank as low as her body had been the week before when the wave pushed her to the bottom of the ocean floor.

Saturday night, Molly was the last to be picked up. She dressed thematically for an eighties rave party in black spandex tights that reached just below the knee, and a pink-and-white-striped knit off-the-shoulder dress from the Goodwill store. She had even colored her hair hot pink in half-inch streaks. She wore big hoop earrings, and huge wedge sandals that grew her height to at least five foot five. Carefully maneuvering down the steps of the trailer, she was disappointed to see AJ at the wheel of his mom's Suburban; she had hoped to see Kai picking her up in his Volvo. Climbing inside, she saw that AJ was also dressed in costume as well, sporting phat pants and goggles, quintessential fashion elements of the eighties rave scene.

Molly smiled. Of course AJ would have the perfect fashion accessories for any kind of party. "Someday I'd like to see the inside of your closet, AJ, because I bet it's just amazing," Molly said.

"It's kinda like Paris Hilton's, only even more organized," Riki said, only half teasing. Her own nod to thematic dressing was a Duran Duran concert T-shirt.

Flea complained to Molly as she climbed in the back beside him that no one had bothered to inform him that it was a costume party. And Buzz worried that he would feel "mondo out of place" in street clothes. Molly apologized, assuring them both that her failure to pass on the info that it was a costume party was an unintentional oversight.

"Where's Kai?" Molly asked, trying to sound casual.

"He's meeting us at the party," AJ explained.

"If he shows up at all," Riki added.

As they drove down Pier Avenue, Molly looked out the window at the downtown crowds and tried to sort out her feelings. Since sunset, she'd experienced the same bubbles of optimism gurgling up inside of her that she felt that night at the Lighthouse. She found it puzzling that her emotions seemed so much more manageable during the daylight hours; she could surf with Kai or talk to him in jazz band. But when the sun set and the moon began to rise, her emotions were colored by the prospect of being with him, even in a group. No, she wasn't certain at all she was prepared to dance this dance of hope, especially not in black tights and a pink-

and-white-striped dress. But as AJ pulled up to Andrea's beachfront mansion, Molly felt the stirrings of possibility rise up in her again and she knew that, for better or worse, hope would be her constant companion.

"You have pink hair," Andrea said, stating the obvious as she greeted Molly and her crew when they entered, gifts in hand.

Inside, a hundred kids were milling around the downstairs foyer and dining area; a hundred more were already dancing upstairs. As Molly scanned the crowd, she realized that she and AJ were the only ones dressed in eighties garb.

"I thought it was a costume party," Molly said.

"Where did you get that idea?" Andrea asked.

"From you," Molly said.

"Oh, Molly, you must have misunderstood. But don't worry about it. You look adorable," Andrea said, welcoming them in.

"Well, I for one am glad I did not receive the costume memo," Buzz said to Flea as they walked in.

Andrea looked stunning in a slinky satin spaghetti-strap blouse with ruffles across the bodice, and a pair of oh-so-tight three-hundred-dollar jeans with a pedigree of their own. Andrea explained how she bought the jeans at a designer store and then shipped them off to a former

Playboy Bunny/porn star/entrepreneur who distressed brand-new jeans for a mere two hundred dollars a pair.

"Next time you want your jeans beat up, just give them to me. Because I am a total expert at screwing up laundry. I bet I have distressed as many perfectly good jeans as your porn star, except I don't charge two hundred dollars. And all I need is a couple of quarters and a box of Tide," Molly said.

Only Flea laughed out loud.

Molly handed Andrea a wrapped present, a cat's-eye necklace from a local surf shop. She had spent over thirty dollars, which was fifteen over her budget.

"Oh. My. God. A real present," Andrea said as she ripped the box open.

She gestured to the table where there were stacks of envelopes, most containing gift cards. Andrea explained to Molly that kids at Beach High didn't generally give presents; they gave gift cards or sometimes even cash. "My mom calls birthday parties at Beach fund-raisers for rich kids."

Like Molly, Waldo also had brought a real present, wrapped in rumpled tissue and stuffed in a floral gift bag with raggedy edges, clearly used before.

"I got you what every girl wants for her sweet sixteen," Waldo said.

Andrea ripped through the tissue. Inside the bag was a round black and red can labeled MR. ZOG'S SEX. Molly explained to Andrea that the canned Sex she held in her hand was, in fact, surfboard wax, a rather stupid insider joke. "Which is not all that funny, I might add."

"Well, he gets points for trying." Andrea said, playing the good hostess.

"Waldo, if dumb was dirt, you'd cover about an acre," Molly said.

"Where's Kai?" Andrea asked casually, trying to mask her disappointment that he had not arrived with the group.

Evidently, Molly was not the only one who danced with hope that night.

Kai knocked on the door of Duke's trailer half a dozen times before he finally roused him. Duke yelled from behind the locked door to leave him alone.

"I'm not going until I make sure you're okay."

"I'm okay, so go," Duke yelled again.

"I'm not convinced," Kai answered. He waited for a long time, listening for signs of authentic life from inside the trailer. Hearing none, he dug in his heels, resolute.

"Are you still there?" Duke asked, barely audible through the locked door.

"Yes, I am. And I'm not leaving until I see for myself how okay you really are," Kai said.

Duke kicked the door open.

Even in the dim light, Kai could see that Duke looked bad; his skin was yellow, and pallid; his hair unkempt, unwashed. He was barefoot and wore rumpled board shorts, but the silk Hawaiian shirt he sported looked like it was fresh from the cleaners.

"Nice shirt. Who's getting married?" Kai asked.

Duke laughed out loud. "It just happened to be hanging on the chair, closest to the door."

"Why haven't you been at class all week?" Kai asked.

"I haven't felt well."

"Have you been drinking?'

"No, and that's the truth," Duke said.

"Well, you look terrible," Kai said.

"I feel terrible," Duke said. "I have the stomach flu. Now, if you'll excuse me, I need to throw up again."

Kai sat on the steps and waited, listening to the awful sounds of Duke retching in the bathroom. He was relieved to hear a flushing toilet, and in a minute, Duke returned, this time carrying a ginger ale.

"It's not your job to take care of me," Duke said, sitting down next to Kai.

"If you screw up again, they'll fire you," Kai said.

Duke didn't make much money as the Surf Ed. instructor and since he was a classified employee instead of a real teacher, he was not subject to the same kind of moral scrutiny as certified teachers. Even with the lax standards, Duke had managed to get himself in a little trouble with the administration. His record on the beach and with the kids was stellar, but being a local hero had its downside; being in the limelight meant he was visible, very visible. Two weeks before school was out last year, it had come to the administration's attention (written up in the local rag) that Duke had been arrested (taken into custody) for disorderly conduct (spitting on the sidewalk).

His run-in with the law occurred at a local surf festival, the culmination of a wild weekend of partying, where arrests doubled and infractions far worse than spitting had been committed. Duke's problems on that evening began with an argument with an off-duty cop who happened to be an old classmate. They hadn't liked each other in high school, and their relationship had not improved over the years. They got into an animated argument over where the best break in the South Bay was, which escalated and moved outside of the bar. Duke shouted that it was El Porto, not Torrance, and to make his point, he spit on the sidewalk. Discussion finished, he walked back inside.

But his old classmate, the off-duty cop, was convinced that some of Duke's spit had landed on his brand-new pair of Bridgeport deck shoes, so he chased Duke back into the bar, cuffed him, and arrested him on the spot for assaulting an officer. Fortunately for Duke, the captain of the Hermosa Beach police force reviewed the initial arrest report and changed the charges from assaulting an officer to disorderly conduct. When the off-duty cop protested, his superior asked him if he wanted to be remembered as the only law enforcement officer in the entire history of Hermosa Beach to have been assaulted by a *spit-and-run*.

In the end, no formal charges were filed at all. But all the brouhaha led to the uncovering of Duke's former and only run-in with the law in Long Beach when he was nineteen. The administration decided that it was unseemly to have a school employee, even if he was just a classified one, written up in the local paper as being disrespectful to a representative of authority, so they put Duke on probation.

Duke knew Kai worried too much about others, himself included, but he didn't want him to feel responsible for his keeping his job.

"Some people are natural-born caregivers. But in your case, I think the role was forced on you because your mother got sick. And you handled it like a man. But just because you took care of your mom and helped her through a hard time doesn't mean that it's now your job to take care of everybody else. Do you understand what I'm saying?"

Kai nodded. Besides Duke, Flea was the only other one

from the Dawn Patrol who knew about the battle Kai's mother waged against breast cancer last year. Kai was as private as he was protective of his mom. His parents had divorced when he was four, and he seldom saw his father. He had two older brothers, one who lived on the big island of Hawaii and one who lived on the smaller Sanibel Island in Florida. "The water runs through them," his mother said about her sons, who were all excellent watermen and could not imagine living anywhere not near an ocean.

"Unlike their father," she always added, who was perfectly comfortable residing in Kansas. After she was diagnosed, the burden of her care fell to Kai because his older brothers were so far away. The experience forced him to mature faster than either mother or son would have preferred; he became even more self-reliant. He was a lot like Molly in that the circumstances of their mothers' lives had thrust them into a stratosphere of independence not often afforded middle-class kids from the suburbs. Simply put, they had grown up early.

The two men sat in silence for a long time, listening to the sounds of the night, the stop-and-go traffic on Valley, the wind coming down off the bluff and rattling the fronds on the tall palm trees, the occasional shriek of a gull.

"Shit happens when you live alone, when there's no

one to look after you," Kai said finally, explaining why he had come to Duke's trailer to check on him.

"Having somebody else in the room won't protect you from shit happening. It just means that when you're knee-deep in it, you'll have company," Duke said, slapping Kai's back, smiling. "Don't worry about me. I like living alone. And you have a party to go to."

Upstairs in Andrea's beachfront mansion, the real party was just getting started. All of the furniture had been moved out of the room, replaced with a portable dance floor the size of a small club. Giant screens projecting tie-dyed bubbles were installed against one wall. The Dawn Patrol was stationed safely on the edges of the dance floor, watching half a dozen theater geeks dancing to the loud, thumping beat. They popped up and down, holding what looked to be invisible balls of energy between both hands, which they shook above their heads.

"This is just like a rave. Except without the drugs," AJ said with authority.

"Speak for yourself," a theater geek screamed as he bounced past, invisible globe in hand and obviously high on something.

Molly had never been to a rave. But she had seen mosh pits, and the kind of dancing she witnessed now more closely resembled that kind of free-flowing kinetic energy than the kind of dancing she was accustomed to. Flea tried to coerce her onto the dance floor with him, but Molly hesitated, afraid of embarrassing herself. Riki pulled Molly aside for a private word. "You have to dance with Flea."

"Why?"

"Because he likes you," Riki said, having no idea of the Kai/dash/Molly drama unfolding just below the surface of the relationship waters.

Molly was stunned. "Did he tell you that?"

"No, Waldo did. And he would know." For all his faults, Waldo was a keen observer of the male condition.

Flea interrupted and grabbed her hand, pulling her onto the dance floor. And this time, Molly acquiesced, deciding that she'd rather dance with Flea than have a conversation about him with Riki.

Dancing with Flea was a revelation. As coordinated as he was uninhibited, he was a master of popping and locking moves that he translated from hip-hop to the more liquid gyrations of the rave scene For her part, Molly moved her head and shoulders to the beat and tried to stay out of his way. When the music got louder and even more frenetic, Flea thrashed his arms and legs forward in opposition to one another like a cross-country skier. The other dancers cleared the floor to give him room, and Molly found herself and Flea at the center of attention. As much as Molly longed to be singled out, to be noticed, to be rescued from the high school ranks of the invisible, dancing with a guy who looked like he was stuck in a time warp on a NordicTrack was not what she had in mind.

"Just follow me. Do what I do," Flea shouted over the music.

"So not possible," Molly said.

"But it's easy. You don't have to count steps or anything," Flea said.

"I can see that," Molly said, watching her dance partner pop up and down like a jack-in-the-box on methamphetamine.

The song thankfully ended, and Molly tried to retreat from the center of attention. But as a slow tune began, Flea stayed her.

"One more dance," he said, turning what should have been a question into a royal command. He slipped his arms around her waist, a bold move for the NordicTrack dancer.

Trapped, Molly put her arms around Flea's neck, purposefully keeping them a little stiff so she could keep an acceptable distance between them. She didn't want to dance too close to him, given the new information from Riki via Waldo, because the last thing she wanted to do what give this incredible guy whom she really liked the wrong impression. But it was too late; he was already too far gone.

THIRTEEN

"LOOK, I APOLOGIZE BECAUSE I DIDN'T BRING A PRESENT OR ANYTHING," KAI SAID to Andrea, taking inventory of the over two hundred gift cards piled high on the credenza as he walked into the party, which was in full swing.

"Like I need another gift card to Blockbuster? I'm just glad you came. Besides, what I really want for my birthday will not fit into an envelope," Andrea said, flirting.

Kai took in the palatial surroundings and couldn't imagine what Andrea might be lacking. "Looks like you already have everything. It's a great house."

She thanked him, and they chatted easily as they wandered through the downstairs rooms. Andrea introduced him to several of her ASB buddies, but she noticed that he was not completely attentive. His eyes drifted away from her, searching the room for someone else. Molly, of course. Andrea had planned to make her move at the end of the evening but, afraid she might not get the chance once he hooked up with Molly, she took his hand.

"Come on, there's something I want to show you."

She led him upstairs, and they skirted past the edge of the dance floor. There, he saw, quite by accident, Flea slow-dancing with Molly, their arms wrapped around each other, deep in what looked to be a meaningful conversation. Kai knew that Flea wasn't a player, and he didn't think Molly was, but maybe he had been wrong. Just as he was about to turn the corner and head down the hallway with Andrea, he caught Molly's gaze. They exchanged a look, sizzling with accusation.

What are you doing with him?

What are *you* doing with *her*?

And that was all that passed between them, a searing glance across a crowded room, a telepathic question that neither had the opportunity to answer. Because in the next second, Flea's hand wandered down Molly's back. And at exactly that same instant in time, Andrea grabbed Kai's hand proprietarily, dragging him away from the party and down the hallway toward her bedroom. If there were such a thing as reverse kismet, Molly and Kai appeared to be in the middle of it.

Andrea gently closed the door to her bedroom, a spacious room with a corner window view of the south-facing beach. Kai shuffled, not all that comfortable alone in the opulent bedroom of a girl he barely knew.

"Sometimes I feel like I'm a walking cliché. Ever heard of 'sweet sixteen and never been kissed'?"

"Not you," Kai said, disbelieving.

"No, but really close," Andrea said honestly.

Andrea told him that everybody assumed she had relationships because she was always busy doing something with someone. But it was beyond embarrassing to be a junior at Beach High and never have been engaged in a serious relationship at a place where even freshmen girls regularly gave guys blow jobs during the nutrition break.

Kai was unaware that there were girls who were giving blow jobs during school hours, but he made a mental note to confirm that fact with Waldo.

"I'm not asking you to be my boyfriend, and I don't want a commitment or anything," she said as she slowly unbuttoned her blouse, revealing a lacy bra underneath all the organdy ruffles.

"What about Molly?"

"What about her?"

"I thought you guys were friends."

"We are. Your point?" she asked. "Besides, it looked like to me that Molly had a little something of her own going on with Flea."

Andrea tossed her frilly blouse on an ottoman and moved toward Kai purposefully. Kai had grown accustomed to being propositioned by girls in designer jeans, but this was the very first time that one of them had taken off a four-hundred-dollar tucked organdy blouse in hopes of a kiss. . . .

Molly finished what was the longest slow dance in the history of the Western world, a slow dance so interminable that she felt as if they had reached all the way back to the eighties and played it out in real time. And throughout the entire song, she kept watching the hallway and waiting for Kai and Andrea to return to the party. But neither made an appearance. Not during that dance or the four more that followed. Molly's stomach became queasier with each passing minute, churning with a creeping sense of betrayal.

Deciding that it would be better to know what was going on than to flail around in a quagmire of perceived disasters, she excused herself from the group and walked down the hallway, passing by the laundry room, only bothering to give that a cursory glance. That was maid territory; Andrea would never set foot in there. She looked into the open door of the media room, where some guys were locked into a "beat 'em up" video game. But Kai was not among them; nor did she expect him to be. He had outgrown his addiction to electronics.

That left one more room. Andrea's bedroom. The door was closed. Molly pressed her cheek against it and listened hard, but all she heard was the thumping of her own heart. Her hands began to sweat. Should she knock? Or just barge right in?

"What are you doing?"

Surprised, Molly flipped around to find Flea looking at her strangely. "You just disappeared. Everyone wondered where you got off to."

"Everyone?" Molly asked.

"Well, me," Flea admitted. "Why are you acting so weird?"

"Because I *am* weird," Molly said, laughing nervously, grateful to be delivered from her own bad intentions. Earlier she had turned down a glass of champagne offered to her by Andrea's mom. Now, she decided, was a good time to have one.

On the patio light-up bar downstairs were three kegs of beer and a magnum of very expensive champagne. Even though Andrea had assured Molly there would be alcohol at the party, it was shocking to see it in plain sight. In her experience, moms did not pop for keggers for their daughter's sweet sixteen and her friends on a well-lit terrace. It wasn't like kids didn't drink at parties in Lubbock, because they did. But they had to sneak it into parties, like by putting vodka in water bottles or at the very least pulling cup sleeves over their beers.

The bartender was on a bathroom break, so Molly served herself. But instead of using a three-ounce flute, she poured the champagne into one of the ten-ounce red plastic cups intended for beer. She downed half of it in one gulp.

"You might want to pace yourself, Molly. A good rule of thumb when you first start drinking is to only have one drink per hour and then stop with two," Flea said, trying to be helpful.

Molly turned her wild eyes on him. "In general, I hate rules of thumb. Almost as much as I hate finger-wagging."

She stomped off and he followed, offering a string of apologies. They started up the steps just as Andrea and Kai were starting down. They met in the middle of the staircase and exchanged awkward pleasantries. It was difficult to tell who was the more ill at ease, Kai or Molly. In contrast, Andrea, who knew everything, and Flea, who knew nothing, seemed perfectly comfortable.

"Hey, brah, you wanna show me where they keep the beer?" Kai asked Flea, and the two guys retreated, leaving the birthday girl and her friend on the stairs. Molly teetered in her high heels; this time she blamed her unsteadiness on the champagne. Molly slipped out of her wedge sandals and dangled them by her finger. Andrea put on a Cheshire-cat grin.

"So are you having a good time?" Andrea asked.

"What were you and Kai doing in your bedroom?"

"God, Molly, what do you think?"

"If I knew what to think, I wouldn't have to ask."

Andrea smiled coyly, playing her moment of meanness for all it was worth. The attention lavished on her all week long, culminating with this outrageously expensive party, had transformed her into something even beyond a spoiled princess of the Beach High set. She had become a birthday glutton. And she used her emerging sense of power to have a little more fun at Molly's expense.

"Kai has the most amazing body, doesn't he?" Andrea asked.

Fighting back angry tears, Molly pushed past Andrea, ran down the stairs and out the front door, leaving her shoes, her pride, her friends, and the guy she thought she could trust far behind her.

Molly ran out onto the walk street, over the cement pathway on the Strand and across the soft sand beach. She didn't stop until she hit the hard-pack by the ocean's edge. The pale light of the beachcomber's moon glittered across a treasure chest of shells exposed by the low tide. Generally, her beach was shell barren, only a few washed up in summers. But with a low tide and an early winter storm brewing in Baja, the beach was awash in shells of every shape and muted color ranging from buttery yellow to soft coral to gray. She walked along the water's edge, picking up shell after shell, examining them with wonder.

Her mother had always said, "When things happen in your life that make you feel like you've been through a car wash in a convertible with the top down, there's only one thing you can do that is guaranteed to make you feel better: Go shopping."

Lynette maintained that nothing could lift a girl's spirits like a new pair of shoes. Tonight, Molly found comfort in that familiar feminine ritual. But instead of perusing the department stores in a mall, she found solace in the magnificently dressed store windows of nature. She went shopping for shells.

The first treasure she found was a white sand dollar the size of the palm of her hand, delicate and perfect, a five-pointed shape on its back. She found a second, hoping to make a pair, but unlike the first, it was still alive. Densely packed, tiny, dark purple spines covered its back, hiding the star design. When she held it in her hand, the spines tickled her palm like a wiry brush. She walked to the edge of the water and released that sand dollar treasure back into the ocean, wishing for it and herself a better turn of fortune. She stayed there for a minute, letting the soft sand squish between her toes as she surveyed her personal shopper's paradise.

"Molly, wait up. What are you doing?"

Molly turned and saw Kai, Andrea, and the entire crew trudging through the sand toward her. At that moment, she wished she had run away in the direction of the hills of Hermosa instead of the ocean shore, to someplace where she couldn't be so easily found.

"For god's sake, Molly, don't be such a drama queen. I was just kidding around. Nothing happened," Andrea said as they reached her.

"Why do you care what Kai and Andrea were doing, anyway?" Flea asked, totally clueless.

Molly and Kai shifted uneasily. An uncomfortable silence fell on the group as if at some level, each of them knew that their interpersonal dynamics were in danger of shifting to a new and bizarre level.

The music from the DJ drifted all the way to the water's edge. Lured back by the party lights, the group trekked through the sand to the Eighth Street entrance. When they reached the boardwalk, they paused so that Andrea could dump the sand out of her Manolo slippers. The houses on the Strand were designed in different architectural styles, ranging from Mediterranean to Spanish to Victorian to Modern to Cape Cod to Craftsman. But what united all of these beachfront mansions were walls of windows, sometimes three stories high. During the day, the blinds were shut tight to ensure privacy because from sunrise to sunset the Strand bustled with activity: pedestrians, runners, skateboarders, and bicyclists paraded up and down the paved boardwalk that ran from Rat's Beach in Redondo all the way to Malibu. But after the sun set, the human traffic thinned, and the drapes were opened so that the owners could take an unencumbered advantage of their pricey views. The combination of floor-to-ceiling windows and inside lights made it possible for the casual passerby to catch an intimate glimpse of how the oh-so-fortunate lived.

Andrea shook the last granules of sand out of her strappy shoes and slipped them back on. When she straightened, she glanced up. In front of her was the corner house on Eight Street, a newly remodeled Cape Cod. Inside, Andrea could see rooms filled with boxes and furniture not quite yet arranged. A young couple unpacked dishes in the kitchen. And sitting on the table in plain view was an infant carrier that held a sleeping baby.

Andrea suddenly realized whose house this was supposed to be. "Molly, what are those people doing in your house?"

Molly stammered, caught off guard. Also on her to-do

list was to plant the seeds of a new lie about the remodel before the old lie was discovered. It would have been so easy to make up a story about having to sell the house. She could have said that it fell out of escrow or that her mother was hoping to reconcile with her father. There were a million excuses, any of which would have been perfectly acceptable if casually dropped at lunch or during nutrition break, but under the scrutiny of *the now*, all of them seemed totally lame. Molly had no real, innate desire to tell the truth, to come clean. She would have preferred to live with her lie through eternity. Yeah, she could have done that. But the problem was, she felt like she could no longer sell the lie.

"That's not my house," Molly said.

"What do you mean? You said the one on Eighth? The remodel? The Cape Cod," Andrea insisted. "This has got to be your house. It's the only one that fits that description."

"It is the house I described. But it's just not *my* house. And it never was."

"Why did you say it was? That is just outrageous, Molly," Andrea said.

Molly struggled to explain herself. "Look, the reason I lied is that I didn't want anyone to know that I live in a trailer park."

"I don't get it," AJ said, typically clueless.

"I do. That place creeps me out," Andrea pointed out.

"Everybody in Texas knows that the first place a tornado hits is the trailer park," Molly said.

Kai looked at her incredulously. "That's your justification? You lied because you felt like a target?"

She didn't know if it was the two glasses of champagne, the conversation with Riki, the dance with Flea, her ambivalence about Kai, or the misunderstanding with Andrea—however you looked at it, she was not having a good night—but each incident stoked the fires of her discontent. She told them that none of them could ever understand what it was like to be her—to be jerked out of her house, forced to leave her life and her dad in the middle of the night, to be torn away from everything she loved and all that was familiar. She had been transplanted, like a desert plant, her roots ripped from the ground and then stuck in the sand at the beach.

"Actually, Los Angeles is a desert too," remarked Buzz, who was a stickler for facts.

"Back home, I went to a real school that had real hallways and a real cafeteria and just plain PE. And I had lots of friends."

Molly stopped. In her forced moment of truth she decided not to complicate matters with yet another lie, so she corrected herself. "Okay, I had two friends. But they were two really good friends. Look, I don't want to talk about this anymore, okay? I lied. I'm sorry. Oh, well. I'm outta here."

She bolted, and this time she headed east toward the downtown area instead of the shore where she would be harder to find.

"You have friends here, too," Flea called after her.

But she didn't hear a word he said.

FOURTEEN

IT WAS PAST MIDNIGHT WHEN MOLLY DITCHED THE PARTY FOR DOWNTOWN HERMOSA. ON her way up the hill, she passed by the old theater, one of the last remaining movie palaces in Southern California. The marquee advertised in neon-colored letters an all-night film festival featuring classic surf films. Not wanting to go home to her empty room, she decided to check it out. She paid admission, bought a bag of stale popcorn, and settled in her seat. And somewhere between *The Endless Summer* and *Riding Giants* she fell into a deep, sound sleep. When she awoke, there were only four people left in the theater. She checked the time on her cell phone; it was almost five. Unconcerned, she yawned, stretched, and headed for the door, leaving the dark night of the theater and stepping out into day.

A light fog wisped through the downtown area, soften-ing the edges of the buildings and muting their normally vivid colors. It was as if her little California beach town had been rendered French by an Impressionist painter. With plenty of time to get home before her mother returned from work, she grabbed a cup of coffee at Java Boy and lazily strolled back to the trailer park, mulling over last night's disaster. The overcast skies matched her mood. She decided that she was worse off now than she was when she first moved to Hermosa, having successfully blown the two real connections she had made at school—Andrea and the Dawn Patrol—with unnecessary lies. How cruel that at the point when her life was looking up, she had single-handedly managed to ruin it?

The events of the last night replayed in her head like a bad movie, which stopped abruptly the minute she turned into the trailer park and saw four police cars parked in front of her home. Terrified that something horrible had happened to her mother while she was sleeping in the movie theater, she ran across the asphalt, broad-jumping the speed bumps. As she neared her front door, she noticed her mother's car pulled up to the side yard at an odd angle. The driver's side door was ajar. Three trailers down, Miz Boyer, wearing a faded floral housecoat and hot pink Ugg boots, paced nervously, wringing her hands. In her thirty-five years as resident and manager, the only hooligans that had caused her any trouble were the seagulls. Never had one police car needed to enter the premises, much less four.

"What's going on in there?" she demanded.

"I don't know. I just got here," Molly screamed back.

Miz Boyer eyed Molly with suspicion as she flew up the steps. Smart-ass girls were always trouble, and this one was more than most.

Molly skidded to a stop at her front door. She had no idea what to expect, but with four cop cars parked outside, she knew enough to proceed cautiously. Her father had always warned her not to make any sudden moves when dealing with men with guns, even those who carried them in an official capacity. With that in mind, she turned the handle cautiously. The door creaked open, and she entered the living room slowly, deliberately, and loudly announcing her arrival, "I'm Molly, and I live here!"

"Oh, thank God," Lynette screamed, almost knocking Molly over as she smothered her with hugs. But Lynette's relief in having found her missing daughter quickly dissipated. Now that she knew Molly was alive, she could be mad; she demanded to know where she had been all night.

"I fell asleep at the surf film festival. But what's with all the cop cars? And what are they doing here" Molly asked, pointing to AJ, Waldo, Buzz, and Flea who were sitting on the sofa with their hands cuffed behind their backs.

Flea opened up his mouth to explain, but Officer Price

bellowed, "Don't even think about it. You don't speak unless spoken to. Got it?"

Flea nodded, not about to argue with the Hermosa Beach version of *Dirty Harry*. Officer Price was a burly man with a hard, chiseled face and an imposing swagger. He longed for the opportunity to tell some unruly suspect to "make my day." Afraid of being carted off to jail, the boys under custody on the couch didn't utter a peep, begging Molly with their eyes to get them out of this mess.

But Molly was in the dark. Lynette explained the sequence of events to her. Officer Price had been driving his patrol car down Valley when he saw four boys, armed with paper bags full of something sneaking into the trailer park. Alarmed, Officer Price parked his squad car, called for backup, and went after them on foot. He followed the suspects to Molly's trailer, where he spotted the three juveniles breaking and entering through the open window in Molly's bedroom. Price notified Molly's mother at work, who rushed home immediately.

"They completely tore up your room, Molly," Lynette said, beside herself. Molly had not seen her mother so upset since the tree incident in Austin.

"They did what?" Molly exclaimed.

Molly flew across the living room to see for herself. How dare they break into her house and mess with her belongings! Molly's bedroom faced the northwest and had a long, narrow window over the bed. Even though it was light outside, her room was still dark. Molly switched on the light and stood in awe. She felt as if she had walked into a dream. She couldn't believe her eyes. Her room shimmered in a metallic glow, transformed into the perfect domicile for the Tin Man.

She had been foiled, literally.

Her entire room—the bed, the pillows, her clock, her iPod, her computer and all the wires, the sneakers in the middle of the floor, her surfboard leaning against the wall—was covered in aluminum foil. All her stuff, even down to the quarters in the coin jar and the casings of CDs, were silver coated. She felt like she had been cast in a reality-TV show, one of those make-over editions, and the celebrity chosen to redecorate her room had been Tim Burton. The only two items in the room that had been spared were *Sleeping in the Shorebreak*, left untouched on the bed, and a photograph of her and her crew on the beach, standing in front of their boards. It was, however, hanging upside down.

Molly returned to the living room, where Price glared at the four terrified suspects, his hand resting on the gun in his holster. Her mother, still shaken by the intrusion, a foil home invasion, paced anxiously, trying to make sense of her daughter being out all night long while four strange boys burglarized her bedroom. "I don't understand, Molly. They say that you're their friend."

Molly stood motionless, letting the word resonate. Friend. Their friend. Molly recognized their effort for what it was: the biggest foil-covered prank in the history of Beach High, an innocuous joke warped into superspeed that represented her rite of passage into the inner sanctum of the group. She might be too chatty or too angry or a downright liar, but this was their screwy way of letting her know that she belonged, that she was part of the group.

"Well, Molly, do you know these boys?" Officer Price asked seriously.

Molly studied them like they were ex-cons in a lineup. She heaved a sigh worthy of a Southern belle and said, "I've never seen any of them before in my life."

Cost of aluminum foil to cover her room: sixty-seven dollars.

Number of man-hours to do it: fifteen and change . . .

The looks on their faces when she denied knowing them: priceless!

All hell broke less. Even after Molly mumbled a "Just kidding," it took half an hour to sort it all out. Molly tried to explain to her mother that foiling her room was a rite of passage, like when the Beach High girls' volleyball team toilet-papered the incoming freshman girls' homes.

Flea offered his own version of events. "We left the party right after Molly. And since we knew she was upset, we thought she'd probably take a walk, so we decided to come over and wait for her. And when she didn't show, after a while, AJ got this idea that we should foil her surfboard. As a joke. So we drove to the Quickie-Mart and bought a dozen rolls of aluminum foil because we weren't quite sure how much it would take to cover her board. When we got back, we popped the screen on Molly's open window and climbed into her room and got to work. As it turns out, less than one roll is way more than enough to cover a long board. We expected Molly back any minute, but when she didn't show, we had some time on our hands and eleven rolls left-over. So we started foiling stuff. And we got more and more into it. In fact, we even made a second trip to the store because we ran out of supplies."

"What did you think when Molly didn't come home? Weren't you concerned?" Lynette asked.

"We were pretty focused on our project," AJ said.

"So what sports team are you kids on?" Officer Price asked, as if he were looking for holes in the alibi of a dangerous suspect.

"I am so not into sports," Molly explained, "but we're all in the same surfing class."

"Surf Ed.?" Officer Price asked, starting to steam.

When Molly nodded confirmation, he shook his head. "I should have known that loser son-of-a-bitch would be involved. I'm not surprised that you boys have found yourself on the wrong side of the law when you have an instructor who spits in its face."

"I'm sure I have no idea what you're talking about," Molly said, concerned how her mother might react to accusations of impropriety regarding her surf instructor.

"Duke Updike spit on my shoes," he said, threatened by the mere memory of it.

That's nothing. He threw up on mine. But Molly kept those thoughts to herself and said, instead, ever so sweetly, "Well, I'm sure he didn't mean to."

After it was all over, Lynette thanked the Hermosa Beach officers for their due diligence but refused to press charges. She felt that to have been handcuffed in her living room for several hours was punishment enough. So she saw the officers to their squad cars and thanked them. As the cop cars sped away, Miz Boyer flagged her down. Poor Lynette had to spend another half hour explaining the entire incident to her landlady, swearing that it would never happen again.

"Don't make promises you can't keep," Miz Boyer said. "Do you know what your daughter does when you're away at work?"

"Molly is going through a hard time right now. But she's a good girl, and I trust her."

"Well, that is the problem with parents today. They trust their kids. They have forgotten that the one fundamental rule of growing up is that kids lie, especially to their parents. And some lie better than others, if you know what I mean," she said pointedly. "I don't like to meddle. And I'm sure you realize that young girls today are much more independent and freer than when I was her age, especially about sex."

"What are you saying? Does Molly have boys over when I'm at work?"

"Oh no, that would be the good news, if it were true. It's much worse than that. She never has friends over at all. The fact is, she's never home. Believe me, this isn't the first time she stayed out all night."

Exhausted, Lynette quietly closed the door to the trailer behind her. Molly rattled on cheerfully as she picked up the living room. "Thanks for not filing charges against my friends. They're good guys, really. Even though they make me crazy about half the time. I bet you're so tired, because

I know I am. What do you say we crash? And then maybe we could go out to eat for whatever meal we wake up for," Molly said, eager to reestablish détente with her mom.

"I don't even know who you are anymore, Molly."

That was all she said before disappearing into her room, shutting the door behind her and doing something she had never done before, not in the entire four months that they had been in California. She called Molly's father. Listening at the door, Molly heard her mother speaking in low whispers. And although she couldn't make out most of the conversation, she did hear her mother say, "Maybe it would be better if she moved back to Lubbock and lived with you."

Molly retreated into her silvery room and slid onto the floor, not wanting to disturb her crushed-tinfoil bedspread and pillows. Two months ago, her mother's entreaty to her father would have been welcome news, an unexpected resolution to what seemed like an insurmountable problem. But now, she had grave misgivings. She had never been initiated into a group in Lubbock like she had been with the guys from Surf Ed.; no one had ever spent so much time and effort to make her feel like she was a part of a circle of friends. And although she still had not completely fallen in love *with* California, she had fallen in love *in* California, twice. First with surfing, and then with Kai. Why is it, she wondered, that people always fall in love right before they have to leave? It was off the Richter scale of unfair.

All afternoon Molly performed acts of penance purposefully designed to regain her mother's good graces: vacuuming, picking up discarded clothes, scrubbing out the tub, and putting away the clean dishes from the dishwasher. At three on Saturday afternoon, Molly answered the knock at the door, surprised to find Kai standing on her front steps. They hadn't spoken since she bolted from the party the night before.

"Look, before you say anything, I want you to know that I'm truly sorry that I made up all that stuff about moving into a house on the Strand," Molly said quickly, wanting to apologize.

"Being truthful is generally on my top-ten list of things I like about a person. Which is why your 'making up stuff' should make a difference in the way I feel about you, but it doesn't."

"How do you feel about me?" she wondered, daring to hope.

"Can we go get a cup of coffee? Because there's a lot we need to talk about."

"I can't leave the premises. I'm pretty much grounded for life," Molly said, unwilling to break the rules of her mother's ultimatum, especially with the threat of deportation looming over her.

After catching a few hours' sleep, Lynette had returned to work to finish the grant proposal she was working on when she was interrupted by the first call from the cops. Before she left, she told Molly in no uncertain terms that she was not to step one foot out of the trailer park.

"So, is it okay if I come in?" Kai asked.

"I'm not allowed to have guys in the house when my mom's not home," Molly said, and then explained what had happened the night before.

Disappointed but understanding, Kai left with a promise that they would talk later. Molly retreated to her room and once again admired the masterful foil handiwork of the Dawn Patrol. And even though her mother had said that Molly's number-one priority was to clean up the mess in her room, Molly couldn't bear to tear it apart, not yet. So instead, she documented her foiled room with her camera and posted the pictures on the Internet. In less than an hour, there was a second knock at the door. She opened it to Kai, who had returned wearing a sheepish grin on his face and holding two lattes in go-cups.

"I was thinking, what if we shared a cup of coffee up there on the dune?" he said, gesturing to the wall of sand that bordered the trailer park. "That way, I won't be in the house and you'll still be on the premises."

"Problem solved," Molly said, shutting the door behind her.

Molly and Kai climbed halfway up the dune and sat down in the soft sand right above a patch of purple ice plants in full bloom. Even though it was late afternoon, the sun was just breaking through the cloud bank.

"So, what's going on with you and Flea?" Kai asked.

"I don't know. What's going on with you and me?" Molly asked back.

"Flea likes you," Kai said.

"I know. He foiled my room," Molly said.

"No, what I mean is, he has real feelings for you," Kai said, uncomfortable even saying it out loud. "He told me last night on the patio when we were getting beers. Which is odd, because guys don't generally talk about this kind of thing with other guys."

"Which is odd because that's all girls *do* talk about. Some girls, anyway. So did you tell him that you liked me first?" Molly asked.

"No, because evidently Flea's been all over you since the day you first showed up at the beach."

"Well, you could have at least said you *saw* me first," Molly offered, referring to their near-meet on the Strand with the marauding skateboarder.

"This is serious, Molly."

188

"I know it is," she said, putting down her latte and lying back in the sand. Having two guys like her at the same time would have been glorious if it weren't so damn terrible.

He lay down next to her, and they discussed the problem of Flea at length. Kai worried that if he and Molly started/continued seeing each other, it would impact the dynamics of the group. Molly didn't want the group to change either, now that she felt apart of it, but there was something she wanted more. And he was lying right beside her.

"What about Riki? Because I heard that you were with her before Waldo was," Molly said, having wanted to know the details of that relationship for a long time. "When did you break up? What happened?"

"We didn't break up, because we were never together. It was just a one-time thing," Kai said.

"But didn't it make it weird with the group when she got together with Waldo?"

"You've got to understand. Riki operates under different rules. She's a total guy on the inside."

For just a moment, Molly wished she, too, were "a total guy on the inside," because evidently at the Eighth Street tower, guys had more freedom than divas in moving from partner to partner. But in her heart, she knew the difference between Kai's relationship with Riki and her situation with Flea was not based on their sex but on the way they approached sex. Flea was a romantic; Riki was decidedly not.

"So I guess it's over with us until I can fix things with Flea," Molly said.

"Yeah. I think it's best if we just do the friend thing."

"I agree."

They sealed their newly established, clearly defined, and totally platonic relationship with a kiss.

Which was their first mistake.

Down in the trailer park, Miz Boyer lugged a heavy sack of trash to the line of cans at the foot of the dune. Ever vigilant, she looked up into the sky, searching for signs of gulls that might swoop down when she lifted the lid to steal a piece of last night's leftovers. The skies were clear, but on the dune she spotted a couple of kids making out. Disgusted, she shook her head and scrutinized the kissing couple. She thought she recognized the girl, but she couldn't be certain. She pulled out her glasses from the pocket of her jacket so she could get a better look. She slipped them on the edge of her nose and looked hard. What gave Molly away was not the messy bun at the back of her head, it was the Toby Keith concert tee she wore. There weren't too many kids in Hermosa Beach, as in none, who sported country-and-western artists across their backs.

Now Miz Boyer knew for sure: The girl making out with the Hawaiian on the top of the hill was the little slut from 66D.

Up on the dune, Molly and Kai, their legs entangled, groped each other unabashedly. That first kiss moved at warp speed, accelerating to a full-scale exploration of each other's bodies. Molly luxuriated in not only the way he made her feel but the way she imagined she felt to him. Proud of her newly toned body, her rippled abs, her slim hips, she welcomed his touch. She arched her back when he slipped his hand inside her shirt. He followed the outline of her bra with his fingers, and then cupped her breast with his hand. And for just a second, she wished she had worn sexier undies. Her mother always said, "A girl should always wear nice panties in case she gets hit by a bus and has to go to the hospital, because they might have to take her clothes off and she wouldn't want to be embarrassed."

Well, Molly never believed in dressing for accidents. But she did wish that she had heeded her mother's advice. Suddenly realizing that to entertain the notion of taking off her clothes on the dune was beyond reckless, she bolted upright.

"I think we'd better slow down," she said, breathing hard.

"I agree," Kai said, equally breathless.

Their moratorium was brief. After about two seconds,

they pounced on each other again, diving back in to passion. She thought kissing at night had its own sweet advantages, but she found kissing in the middle of the afternoon with the sun beating down on her back deliciously hot.

Back in the trailer park, Miz Boyer moved from her station at the garbage cans to her front porch, where she still had a clear view of the couple making out on the sand dune. Her porch was a jungle of plants. She sat on a lawn chair, sipping a tall glass of iced tea, unsweetened. Half hidden by a hanging basket of begonias, she kept an eagle eye on Molly and Kai.

Duke ambled through the double-wides, back from the store with a six-pack of ginger ale and two cans of chicken broth. Miz Boyer motioned him over, and he paused for what he hoped would be a short conversation.

"Look who's up on the hill making out with some guy. And he's not one of the ones who broke into her trailer. This one's browner than those other guys. And I don't think it's all tan."

Duke flinched at her racist remark. "Maybe you should go inside and turn on your TV and watch something more PG," Duke said.

"Are you going to tell her mother what goes on here while she's at work?"

"No, and neither are you," Duke said emphatically.

"You do what you like, but I have a moral and legal responsibility as manager of this trailer park to maintain standards of propriety," Miz Boyer said, shaking the ice in her glass.

"For ten years I have ignored my moral and legal responsibility as a good citizen of this trailer park to call the authorities and tell them that you grow weed," he said, gesturing to a pot of cannabis on her front porch behind large cymbidium with fragrant white blooms.

"You wouldn't!"

"I might."

"That is medicinal marijuana. I have bad knees," Miz Boyer said, highly offended.

"I'm sure it is. Look, we're all bozos on the same bus, *Miz* Boyer. So why don't you move to the back of it and leave those two kids alone. They're not hurting anybody."

FIFTEEN

KAI AND MOLLY WALKED DOWN FROM THE DUNE HAND-IN-HAND IN AN AWKWARD having exhausted the afternoon in the most intense and amazing make-out session Molly had ever experienced. Their best intentions flung aside, they now grappled with the repercussions of their passion. When they reached the steps to her trailer, Kai stammered, "You wanna talk about what just happened up there on the dune?"

"Not really," Molly said honestly.

"Good. Neither do I," he said. "But we have to agree to not let it happen again. Not until you resolve the whole Flea thing."

"Agreed. And you have to leave now before my mother gets home and I get into more trouble."

Kai nodded and leaned in to kiss her good-bye, but this time Molly pulled back, afraid that if his lips touched hers just one more time, she would pull him to the ground and do him right there on the steps of the trailer.

"At the risk of talking about that which we agreed not to talk about, I'm thinking a good-bye kiss will end up a 'Hello, here we go again.'"

"Right. See ya," he said, and instead, gave her a friendly little punch on the shoulder as he walked away.

The first time Kai kissed her, Molly let the taste of him linger on her lips, but this time and so many kisses later, she headed straight for the showers, certain that the smell of him was strong on her body. So strong that her mother would know what she had been up to the minute she walked in and put down her purse. Molly was still in the shower thirty minutes later when her mother dropped her shoulder bag by the front door. It landed with a soft thud.

While Lynette started dinner, Molly pulled two of the Irish rose dinner plates from the cabinet, the ones her mother decided not to sell on eBay.

"Thanks for cleaning up the house while I was gone, but do not think for one minute that scrubbing out the tub buys you a 'get out of jail free' pass," Lynette said.

Molly, as frustrated with her mother as her mother was with her, said, "I don't know what you want from me."

"And I don't know what to do with you. You're too young to be out all night, and you're too old for a babysitter.

I have to be able to trust you," Lynette said as she chopped tomatoes.

"You can," Molly insisted.

Lynette arched her eyebrow. "Not according to what happened last night, I can't."

"Okay, so maybe you can't trust me to do exactly what you want me to do. But you can trust me to make good decisions. And I think that's more important," Molly said.

Lynette created her own list of worst-case scenarios of what could happen to a sixteen-year-old wandering the streets of Hermosa at night. "You could end up in over your head, pregnant, or into drugs."

"Mom, I could get into drugs or knocked up at school during third period."

"You have to stop wandering around at night or else—" Lynette said, her voice wavering.

"Or else what? You gonna ship me off to Lubbock?" Molly asked.

Molly told her mother that she had overheard their phone conversation. It had occurred to Molly that if her father was involved with someone else, he might not even want her to live with him. Keeping her fears and her suspicions to herself, she asked her mother if her father still wanted her.

"He said that you were always welcome to live with him

but that it had to be your decision. He didn't want me to force you into anything."

The thinly veiled threat of deportation lifting, Molly mustered every ounce of courage in her and returned to the one question that had been bothering her for such a very long time.

"Why would you send me back to a place where you couldn't bear to be?"

Lynette looked at her daughter, measuring her words as carefully as she measured the cup of tomatoes that she threw in the saucepan.

"He may be an asshole, but he's still your father and he loves you."

They were interrupted by a knock at the door.

"It's probably Miz Boyer," Lynette said.

"I'll get it," Molly said as she flew out of the kitchen before her mother could put down the wooden spoon she used to stir the marinara sauce.

Molly opened the door. Standing outside on the small stoop was Flea, wearing cargo shorts and a Hawaiian shirt, his hair spiked, which added another inch to his height. In his arms he held an enormous bouquet of yellow roses, just like the ones on Molly's boots. Molly burst into tears and slammed the door in his face.

Shocked by her outburst, Flea stood paralyzed on the

stoop, limply holding the impressive bouquet of roses that had cost him his last forty dollars, and wondering what to do next. After a moment, the door creaked open and Molly reappeared, composed and dry-eyed. Lynette hovered behind, holding a stained chili-pepper print pot holder.

"I'm sorry, Flea. But I'm a little emotional tonight," Molly offered as way of an explanation.

"I didn't mean to weird you out," Flea said sheepishly.

"I'm not used to getting flowers. I didn't know how to react," Molly said.

"Relax. They're not for you. They're for your mom," he said, handing them to Lynette. "Thank you for being so understanding. They had red ones too, but I thought it'd be cool to get you yellow roses because you're from Texas."

"You know about 'The Yellow Rose of Texas'?" Lynette asked.

"Yes, ma'am. I think it's a song or something," Flea said, hoping he was making a better impression than he had this morning handcuffed on her couch.

"Well, no one has ever given me yellow roses before, and they are lovely, but I don't know quite what to make of the comparison. Do you actually know who the Yellow Rose of Texas was?" Lynette asked.

"Uh, no, ma'am."

"Mom, please . . . do you have to?" Molly pleaded.

Unlike Flea, Molly was a well-bred Texas girl and knew the story.

Ignoring her daughter, Lynette devoted her sole attention to Flea. "The Yellow Rose of Texas was an indentured servant during the Texas Revolution. Legend has it that she seduced the famous Mexican general, Santa Anna, with a champagne breakfast on the morning of the historic Battle of San Jacinto."

Both Molly and Flea flinched at the mention of "champagne." If she noticed, Lynette made no indication. She continued with her story. "While he was busy with *breakfast*, the Texas army launched a surprise attack. Santa Anna was caught off guard and with his pants down. He lost the battle, and the bid for Texas. Some say the Yellow Rose was a true heroine of the Texas Revolution. But others say she was just a whore."

"My bad," Flea said apologetically. "I should have gone with the gerbera daisies."

"Would you like to come in?" Lynette asked, a thin smile appearing.

Flea stepped inside the trailer gratefully but when Lynette offered him a seat on the sofa, the same one he had occupied that very morning, he hesitated, the memory too fresh. "If it's okay with you, I'll sit there," he said, pointing to a chair.

Molly couldn't stand the thought of the three of them sifting through small talk, and didn't entirely trust her mother to keep the conversation polite. "Mom, I really need to talk to Flea, so we're going to go to my room."

Lynette ushered her daughter into the kitchen for a private word. After everything that had happened, did Molly really think she was going to leave her alone with a boy, even one who had brought roses?

"Look, we'll keep the door open. Nothing's going to happen. I swear. We're not going to drink or do drugs or have sex. I just really need to talk to him about some stuff."

"What stuff?"

"Personal stuff," Molly answered.

Lynette shrugged. "I don't know if I'm just getting old or tired, but go ahead. And keep the door WIDE open."

Flea plopped down on the floor, and Molly joined him after she turned on her bedside lamp and threw a scarlet scarf over it, casting a red glow to her silver-coated room.

"Foiling my room was the weirdest and coolest thing anyone has ever done to me, especially after the way I've acted. I've done terrible things. I have a confession to make," Molly said, prepared to tell him everything, including what she and Kai had done on the dune that very afternoon.

"Are you Catholic?" he asked.

"No, why do you ask?"

"Because confession's a Catholic thing. Jews aren't really into it."

"But Jews are into guilt, right?" she asked.

"Please. We invented it," Flea confirmed. "Which is why we also had to create a ceremony to get rid of it. Ever heard of the Tashlich?"

Molly shook her head, so Flea explained. "It happens every year on Rosh Hashanah, the Jewish New Year. Jews go to the ocean or a stream or a river—anywhere there's fish—and throw bread crumbs on the water. The bread crumbs represent the sins of the last year, which the fish devour. Then you promise to do better in the next."

"So you lose the baggage of last year's mistakes?" Molly asked.

"Exactly. And then the rabbi says something about owning up to the fact that just like fish that swim freely and can get caught up in a net, we, too, can get caught up in our net of sin. Or a lie . . ."

"Do you think you have to be Jewish to participate?"

"Feel free to borrow the idea. I'm sure the rabbi won't mind."

"So can I use just any old bread crumbs, or do they have to be special?" she asked.

"Oh, they have to be very special. You have to pick a type of bread that fits the crime. For instance, if you have ordinary sins, you use white bread. For more complex sins, try multigrain. And if you're guilty of too much irony, you go with rye."

"And I guess that means Waldo would have to atone for too many bad jokes with corn bread."

"You're good to go," Flea said, and then turned serious. He took her hand and turned it over in his own. "I really like you, Molly."

It would have been the perfect time for Molly to set their relationship straight, to let Flea know that she saw him a friend and nothing more. But after the flowers, and the story, and the look on his face, all she could muster was, "I like you, too, Flea."

Listening from the hallway, in earshot of Molly's room but out of her daughter's sight line, Lynette tiptoed back to the kitchen, fearing that Miz Boyer's accusations had been well founded. After all, she heard Molly admit that she "had done terrible things." Worried, Lynette drained the soggy fettuccine into a colander and sighed; they were five minutes past al dente.

Two days before Christmas, the first storm of winter hit Hermosa Beach hard. It poured all night long, and by

Christmas Eve, the sheets of rain had turned the sidewalk gutters into raging rivers, at places three feet wide. Molly ran to the grocery store for her mom to pick up a can of cranberry sauce and even though she wore a parka, she got soaked. She didn't mind. Molly was very happy to momentarily leave the state of California climate and return to something more akin to Texas weather. Rain had become a distant memory in this place where ocean mist counted as precipitation, and she missed the feeling of hard, driving raindrops that stung when they hit her skin. Her IM board was full of chatter that morning; the entire crew was buzzing about building surf conditions. If the rain stopped and there wasn't too much runoff from the city streets polluting the water and closing the beaches for swimming, the surf could be awesome.

The phone was ringing when Molly stepped back inside the trailer. She ran to answer it before the intrusion woke her sleeping mother. It was her dad, calling to wish her a Merry Christmas. He asked her if she had given any more thought to moving back to Texas.

"I don't know, Dad. I miss you and I miss Texas but I've made friends here now."

They chatted easily for a few minutes. Molly told him that she'd gotten the box of gifts he'd sent but she hadn't opened it yet.

"Well, your big Christmas present isn't in the box, which is why I called. How would you like to go to Hawaii over spring break?"

Excited, Molly stifled the urge to scream, not wanting to wake her mom. "Can I bring my board?"

"Of course. We've rented this enormous beachfront house just north of Waikiki."

"What do we need a big ol' house for? Just the two of us."

Even as she said it, she was fearful of the answer.

"Look, Molly, this is a little awkward and I really wanted to wait and tell you in person, but Bridget thought it would be better if you heard it over the phone first."

While her father rattled on about the trip, trying to sell her on the idea of how wonderful it would be to spend the holidays in a tropical paradise, Molly concentrated on the blinking bubble lights on their four-foot Christmas tree, questions swirling through her mind.

Bridget? Was she the same woman who'd had answered her father's phone? The one with the Scandinavian accent? And wouldn't a woman named Bridget be more comfortable plunging into cold snow from a hot sauna rather than into the warm waters of Waikiki?

Molly peppered her dad for details, asking him how long they'd been dating and how old she was. But he was evasive; all he could say was how much Molly was going to like her.

"Thanks, Dad, for the offer, but I'm not sure I'm totally comfortable with the idea of going on a trip with just the two of you."

"Don't worry. Her three kids are going too. She has an eight-year-old daughter who's already four feet seven—if you can believe that—and eleven-year-old twin boys who look like linebackers."

Molly swallowed. She supposed she should be relieved that Bridget was old enough to have three children, but she was surprised that her father would date a woman with any children at all, much less three of them. He had never been particularly fond of kids; he used to joke that the only reason he tolerated Molly was because she was his. She closed her eyes and tried to imagine herself surrounded by a family of statuesque Swedes. By Easter, the eight-year-old might be taller than Molly.

"Thanks so much for asking me, Dad, but if you don't mind, I think I'd rather wait to meet your girlfriend until it gets serious."

"It *is* serious, Molly."

"How serious?" Molly asked, certain that those four months were not nearly enough time for her dad to be in committed relationship. Except for that incident with the trees, her father was not an impulsive man. He lived his life in a calculated, measured way, like the engineer he was.

"We're getting married in April. That's why we want you to come to Hawaii with us. So you can be at the wedding."

Outside the window, telltale flashes of lightning in the southern horizon signaled the onslaught of the second storm system following on the heels of the first, working its way up from Baja.

Even though it was the middle of the afternoon, Molly climbed into bed beside her sleeping mother. She listened to the raindrops beating hard on the flat roof of the trailer, the occasional rumble of faraway thunder. Her brain was spinning fast, performing mental somersaults. She felt unstable, like she was trying to maintain balance on a rocking boat in turbulent seas. And there in her mother's bed, she escaped from the tumult of her real world, from the worst Christmas Eve ever, and fell into a deep, sound afternoon slumber.

SIXTEEN

"IF YOU GO TO HAWAII, I'LL TELL YOU WHERE TO SURF ALL THE BEST BREAKS," KAI TOLD her as they stood on the beach on a bright January morning, the first day back from winter break. The sky was laced with cotton candy clouds, wispy pink streaks across the horizon. He didn't see why Molly was so out of sorts. He'd endure a wedding, a funeral, or an eight-hour bout with botulism if it meant the opportunity to surf the Pipeline once again.

He, Molly, and the rest of the crew surveyed the conditions from the Strand. The third and biggest storm of the season had blown up from Mexico, and four days of torrential downpours, offshore winds, and a ten-foot swell had formed the best waves of the season, maybe even the decade. But the breakers were fierce, and the chalkboard at the lifeguard station posted a warning in big bold letters:

CONDITIONS HAZARDOUS—
ONLY FOR THE EXTREMELY EXPERIENCED

The guys argued over who had the balls to get past those breakers. Molly didn't say a word. She knew that if she tried to ride those waves, she'd die. She suspected that deep down inside, the guys knew it too, which was why they were willing to waste precious water time discussing who among them had the *cojones* to actually do it. Regardless, they were obligated to wait for Duke and let him make the call.

"Race all you bums to the water," Buzz screamed as he hopped onto the cement wall that separated the mansions on the Strand from the sandy beach.

"It'll be a short race," Molly noted. The surf was high, and half the beach was under water. "And you'll win."

"Because I'm so fast," Buzz said, lifting up his shades.

"Not really, but those long, toothpick legs of yours give you a decided advantage in the soft sand."

Everyone laughed, including Buzz. Molly had earned the right to insult them; she was part of the group now. The seven friends tucked their surfboards under their arms and jumped on the wall. On Kai's count, they leaped on the sand and careened toward the water's edge. As Molly predicted, Buzz got there first. The recent ten-foot swells had built up a lot of sand on the beach, and the waves were dumping pretty hard at the surf line. A breaker tumbled toward them, and Waldo let out a stream of obscenities as the foam churned up a busted surfboard that flew across the hard-pack like a Frisbee. He jumped out of harm's way just as the board crashed past him. Concerned, the others instinctively spread out across the sand, scanning the horizon, searching for a sign.

A broken, unleashed board could only mean one thing.

At first Kai thought what he saw was a floating bed of kelp, but when the wave broke, he knew for sure. "We got a surfer facedown," Kai screamed, spotting a body in between the breaks in no-man's land, where the surf was pounding hard.

There were no guards on duty yet. They were just now opening up the main station. He ordered Flea to run down the beach and get help.

"We have to go in after him," Molly pleaded as she slipped out of her sweats. "If we wait for a guard, he could die."

"He's probably dead already," Waldo said, grabbing her arm to stop her.

He knew that none of them, not even the masterful waterman, Kai, was experienced enough to attempt a rescue in these treacherous waters. Molly read the fear on their faces and ignored their warnings. She shook off

Waldo, grabbed her board and, in her indomitable, impulsive fashion, she, the least experienced of them all, plunged into the brink. Kai ran in the opposite direction across the sand and up the ramp to the lifeguard station. He kicked open the locked door.

Meanwhile, Molly let the first wave of the set roll over her. She duck-dived under the second and somehow managed to hold on to her board. She grabbed the rails and paddled, keeping the nose headed into the oncoming surf. Twenty feet from the surfer, Molly disappeared under the next mountainous wave; it sprayed a billow of mist over her. She surfaced and tried repeatedly to power through the surf to get to him, but she got stuck in the impact zone. Molly knew that when a surfer was facedown, every second counted. She herself had been knocked over by a powerful surge and had stared at the sandy ocean floor, had felt her lungs fill with water. Now they filled with fear. For the unknown surfer. And for herself.

"Damnit, Molly," Kai yelled as he followed his friend into the water carrying a pilfered yellow plastic rescue can from the lifeguard station and joining her on what he was certain was a fool's race to save a dead man.

At the lifeguard section station at the pier, the on-duty guard, Archie, unlocked the door to the bright yellow emergency truck. Unlike the busy summer when every lifeguard stand had a guard on duty, during the winter months only a few key stands were manned. Instead, the guards used trucks to patrol stretches of beach, keeping an eye for swimmers or surfers in trouble. Thankfully, when the waves were this big, few actually ventured in; most came to the shore to gawk at the giants, not to surf them. Archie stepped on the running board of the truck and saw Flea racing down the beach toward him, waving his arms and screaming at the top of his lungs, "Surfer down! We got a surfer down!"

Molly felt the sea rise beneath her, lifting her toward the heavens before catapulting her off her board and plunging her into the abyss. The board flailed above her head under water; she grabbed the leash, pulled the board toward her, and held on to the rail. She forced her way through the churning water, desperate for a gasp of air and as she broke the surface, she was bumped sharply by what felt like someone's head and arm.

The surge had unexpectedly propelled her next to the unconscious surfer. Grasping her surfboard with one arm, Molly grabbed up under his armpits and heaved with all her might, jerking his head out of the water. The rush of adrenaline imbued her with super powers, as in the tale of the diminutive grandma who miraculously lifted the front bumper of a two-ton truck to save her trapped granddaughter. His head flopped back on her shoulder and she came face-to-face with the man in the water.

The drowning surfer, the one whose life she now held literally in her hands, was none other than Duke. As far as she could tell, he wasn't breathing; his face was purple, and white stuff was trickling out of his nose. The next wave buckled up to full height, but they slid right under it. She spotted Kai swimming toward her, so she tried to maintain her position, treading water and cradling Duke in her arms until Kai could reach her. Molly considered the fact that Duke was only wearing trunks, not a wet suit, which was odd. Nobody went out into the ocean in January without a wet suit. And she realized then that she wasn't wearing one either; there hadn't been time to change into hers. The water was frigid; her teeth chattering.

"Oh, God, no," Kai screamed as he reached Molly and saw for himself who she held in her arms.

"Help me get him on the surfboard," Molly said.

"It's too risky to paddle him back to shore," Kai yelled back as they were hit dead on by another wave. This wave was more forgiving, and luckily they rose up over it. Kai shoved the yellow rescue device, a floating buoy tied to a rope, through the water toward her. Once she had hold of it, he dove under, unleashed her board, and released it, pushing it down current so as not to interfere with the rescue.

Molly hugged Duke under his rib cage so that his face was thrown back over her shoulder and above the waterline. With the other arm, she clung to the yellow can that kept them buoyant; it was attached to a harness around Kai's chest. Kai stroked down the face of a wave that curled and swallowed them whole. The three disappeared from view of the shore just as Archie's truck ground to a halt in the soft sand. He had radioed ahead, calling for backup and paramedics. He flung open the door and jumped out of his truck, with his own yellow can in hand. Waldo ran up to him, pointing to the spot where they had last surfaced, explaining that Kai and Molly had gone in to rescue the drowning man.

"Oh, great. Now I've got three victims instead of one," Archie said angrily.

Archie barreled across the sand and into the water just as Kai broke the surface and floated up on top of the wave as it began to break. He took two strong pulls, cutting his arms into the water like swords. He positioned his body into a streamline and then kicked like crazy and managed to stay in front of the wave. The size and surge of the wave was powerful enough to launch him toward the shore, dragging Molly and Duke in behind him. Archie dove under the wave as Kai rode it in so he could reach Molly, who was clinging to Duke and the can in a death hold. He looked in the face of his old friend and surfing buddy and turned away briefly. He was the one person Archie knew who could handle a winter storm; he'd ridden out dozens before, many more tumultuous than this one.

"Give him to me, Molly. I've got him now," Archie said, and took the unconscious Duke from her. Without Duke's weight dragging her down, Molly flew up the face of the wave, out of the impact zone. She tumbled toward Waldo, who was standing in knee-deep water with the others, struggling to maintain position in the strong current. He grabbed her arm and jerked her up to her feet. She doubled over, coughing up seawater; Waldo held tight to her shoulder until she could regain her balance.

Archie with Duke in tow crested the next wave and rolled into shore. Together with Kai, Waldo, and Molly's help, Archie hauled Duke's motionless body to the shore. He immediately began to work on him. Archie turned Duke on his left side to help get the water out of his lungs, but only a small amount of salt water dribbled out of his mouth. The Dawn Patrol gathered around and looked on anxiously, holding on to one another, fighting back tears.

"Why isn't more water coming out?" Waldo asked.

"Maybe his larynx is spasmed shut," Archie said. There were no marks on Duke's body or face, nothing to indicate that he had been knocked unconscious.

"Maybe he got caught on the bottom and inhaled water," Kai speculated.

A fire truck with paramedics careened across the sand, answering Archie's distress call for backups. Archie yelled at the two paramedics as they unloaded out of the truck, "I need a V-bag, pronto!"

They grabbed the hand pump from the truck and brought the resuscitator with a bag valve mask, which they attached to Duke in an attempt to start aggressively getting air into his lungs. There were three guys working on him now, but despite their efforts, Duke's chest wasn't moving. He was cyanotic, blue from the lack of oxygen in his blood. They suctioned the inhaled salt water from his mouth and attached a defibrillator to his chest to analyze his heart rhythm.

"I've got a carotid pulse," Archie said.

"I've got a radial pulse, too," the paramedic confirmed.

They had pulse, but still no breath. "Keep bagging him," Archie instructed the paramedics. They worked on him for several minutes. Waldo, Kai, AJ, and Flea kept it together, but just barely. Riki cried openly, but Molly was numb; she no longer felt cold. She didn't feel anything at all. It was only when Flea wrapped a beach towel around her shoulders that she noticed she was shivering uncontrollably, whether from shock or the onset of mild hypothermia, she didn't know or care. All of her energy was focused on the man lying in the sand.

"I don't think he's coming around. I think we're losing him," Archie said.

A wave of despair as gigantic as the real ones crashing on the shore behind them settled in. This was not the ending any of them could have imagined. It had been a successful rescue. He should be safe now, lying in the soft sand warmed by the morning sun, not slipping further away. Molly remembered the words that Duke had said to her when the sea lion was trapped in the rocks, how he had told her that there were times when you could do nothing to save someone. His words resounded now: "Sometimes you have to let them go."

Molly dropped down to the sand, kneeling by Duke's side. She clenched her eyes shut, willing him to live. She prayed for his survival, making deals with God. She promised to quit being so hard on her mom, to give up Kai, to go to her dad's wedding. She even vowed to never tell another lie again, unless of course she really had to. Deal after deal, promise after promise, if only God would let him live.

She felt the gentle touch of Kai's hand on her shoulder. She opened her eyes and thought she saw Duke's chest rise imperceptibly.

"Keep pumping," Archie demanded.

Duke's head moved, just a fraction of an inch. Despair gave way to hope, and the paramedics continued CPR until his breathing became regular and strong. An ambulance skidded to a stop on the bike path of the Strand, its siren howling.

Duke still had not regained consciousness. The paramedics rolled him over to check for spinal injuries. If Duke had been hit by his board and severed his spinal cord, or thrown onto the ocean floor and broken his neck, he wouldn't have been able to lift his head out of the water, to get back to shore. That would explain how a man of his ability and knowledge had gotten into so much trouble. Unable to tell for sure, they immobilized him, placing him on a backboard with a neck brace. They taped his head so that he could not move; his arms were strapped to his side. Archie covered him with blankets. Rather than put him on the lifeguard truck to move him up the sand, they decided that with six men, it was just as easy and perhaps even quicker to carry Duke on the board to the ambulance that was waiting on the bike path.

Up on the Strand, Molly and Kai watched as the paramedics situated Duke in the back of the ambulance. Kai asked Archie if he and Molly could ride to the hospital in the back of the ambulance with Duke.

"You guys go on to school. We'll handle everything from here."

"What about his family?" Kai asked.

"All he has is a sister in South Carolina, but I'll call her," Archie said.

"His real family is right here on the beach. We should be there," Molly said.

Her words trumped protocol. Before swinging the door shut, Archie called out, "Meet us at Torrance Memorial."

"What do you think they're doing? What could be taking so long?" Molly asked Kai anxiously in the waiting room of the emergency room of Torrance Memorial, where they had been stewing for over an hour.

"Everything takes a long time at a hospital," Kai said, speaking from experience.

Molly grew more agitated by the minute and slightly annoyed by Kai, who seemed unnaturally calm. "Aren't you scared? What if he broke his back? What if he's paralyzed? Who will take care of him?"

Only too familiar with the intricacies of navigating hospitals and doctors' offices, Kai had learned that it was better not to speculate, to take bad news one step at a time.

Although they had stopped to change into street clothes before coming to the hospital, Molly's head was still wet and the room felt chilly as if the air conditioner were on instead of the heater. On the beach she had shivered from the icy water but felt nothing. Now she felt like she was freezing to death.

"Is it cold in here or is it just me?" Molly asked.

Even though Kai was chilled too, he took off his own sweatshirt to give to her and wrapped his arms around her to warm her up. Almost immediately, she fell asleep, drifting into the same kind of nothingness she'd found when she napped in her mother's bed after she heard about her father's impending marriage. Lately, she never remembered her dreams and she was grateful for it. She preferred to escape into unencumbered darkness, to a place where bad news could not touch her.

Tumbling into the sweet refuge of slumber, Molly began to snore. She made a peculiar sound like a kitten yawning. Kai thought it was kind of cute, but when the others in the waiting room began to stare, he eased Molly down on the couch so that her head was now resting in his lap. He thought that if he changed her position, she might stop snoring. Wrong! It got worse. The volume increased, and instead of a purring kitten, she sounded like a Harley-Davidson going over Niagara Falls.

Just then the automatic doors opened and Archie emerged. Kai nudged Molly awake. The first thing she noticed was that she was lying on Kai's lap; the second thing was that his pant leg had a wet spot, where she had obviously drooled on him. She wiped away the remaining spittle from her chin and sat up, trying to get her bearings as Archie approached.

"Duke's okay. He's going to be fine. There was no spinal injury; it's the best we could have hoped for," Archie said.

But Molly thought Archie's voice was laced with concern instead of full of relief. In short, he was not very convincing.

"Can we see him?" Molly asked.

"He says you should go to school. He needs to rest. He's really not up to visitors. They may keep him the night, but I'm sure they'll release him by tomorrow morning at the latest."

"Well, tell him we were here. And I'll check in on him tomorrow," Kai said.

As they stood to leave, Archie admonished them for attempting a rescue on their own. Both of them knew how risky it was to go into the water without a lifeguard present.

"Everything worked out this time, but it could have had disastrous consequences. So I want you to promise to never try a rescue like that again, not in those conditions and certainly not on my watch," Archie warned, returning to the ER.

He only took three steps before turning back around and adding, "Having said that, getting to him when you did probably saved his life."

SEVENTEEN

IN THE PARKING LOT, KAI ABSENTMINDEDLY BRUSHED OFF THE WET SPOT ON HIS SHORTS as he climbed into the front seat. Embarrassed, Molly quickly apologized as she slipped into the passenger's side. "Sorry, I think I drooled on you."

"Do you know that you snore?" he asked.

"So I've been told."

"You do this cute little kitten sound when you're all curled up on your side. But when you lie on your back, you sound more like a whale farting."

How romantic! Molly pulled the door shut, making a mental note to never fall asleep in a guy's lap in a crowded hospital waiting room ever again. As Kai turned the key in the ignition, she thought about how basically unromantic their relationship really was. Flea had brought flowers to her house; even AJ had given her a wet suit. Kai had basically given her nothing but a hard time. And yet . . .

Her reverie was interrupted when Kai, seized by an impulse, slammed his foot on the brake as he was backing out and threw the gear shift into park. The engine still running, he leaned over and kissed her hard. It was an explosion of passion, similar to what had happened on the sand dune. She wrapped her arms around his neck and crawled across the seat, straddling the gearshift as she kissed him back. They spent five minutes in a delicious celebration of survival and life—making out in the front seat of Kai's wagon.

Out of the corner of her eye, Molly saw a security officer strolling across the parking lot in their direction. She slid off Kai and back into the passenger seat. When he reached over to kiss her again, she gently pushed him away, nodding in the direction of the approaching parking lot patrolman.

"We'd better get back to school," she said, wiping her mouth and wishing she had a breath mint. But her stale, sleepy breath hadn't seemed to bother Kai, who threw the Volvo into reverse.

"Do you know who else you remind me of, Molly?" Kai asked as he pulled out of the parking lot.

Molly was almost afraid to hear the answer.

"Crocodile Dundee," he said, referring to a character from a favorite movie classic with the surfing set.

"If you're going to keep comparing me to people, could you at least pick someone a little closer to my own age? At least Judi was the right sex."

"No, wait—you're going to like this comparison," Kai said.

"I am so unconvinced," Molly responded.

"Listen before you decide. Dundee was a fish out of water coming from one culture and thrown into another. Just like you, right? And he was brave and outspoken. Again, just like you. But the thing about you that reminds me most of him is that even when you become a part of something, you manage to stay separate from it. You are and will always be a diva on the outside."

Now that sounded romantic.

Word traveled fast at Beach High, but good stories made the rounds faster than the speed of lightning. When Molly returned to school, she received a hero's welcome. And Kai fueled the fires of stardom. Like a shaman around a campfire, he described the details of the early morning surf, the discovery of the body floating near a ball of kelp. He downplayed his part in the rescue, preferring to make her the lone heroine. She was the one who went into the treacherous waters first; she reached Duke first. She brought his face out of the water; she got him to shore; she saved his life.

By ten o'clock, the halls buzzed with the story that Molly had battled six-foot waves to save the life of her surf instructor, and strangers called out a hello during the passing period. At fourth period the swells had grown to ten feet, and Jenn, the senior who had falsely labeled her a lesbian, stepped aside so Molly could get to her locker, pretending to have liked her all along. By lunchtime the legend had grown to twenty-foot breakers, and five different girls invited Molly to parties the next weekend. She basked in all this new attention with the firm conviction that it was well deserved, that she had made a difference; she and Kai had saved a life. As Andrea elbowed her way into the fawning group, Molly told her story for the hundredth time.

"When you're in the trough of a wave as big as the ones were today, there's a point where you can't see the shore and you can't see the horizon. Your whole world is squeezed in between two six-foot walls of water."

Even Andrea was impressed. "Were you afraid?"

"More like terrified. But at the same time, it was like the biggest high ever. You know that old saying that 'you never feel more alive than when you're close to death'— well, that goes triple when you're in the seas after they've been torn up by a winter storm."

• • •

After school the tuba-playing freshman approached her timidly and offered her one of his three highly regarded packages of Ding Dongs that he had saved back from lunch. Realizing that she hadn't eaten all day, she took it gratefully and thanked him. Molly walked away, realizing as she ripped open the package of sugary confection that this was possibly their first real connection.

When she got home, her mother was wide awake waiting for her, which was odd because she usually didn't get up until closer to six. But a reporter from one of the local newspapers had called asking for a quote, which is how she learned that her daughter had risked her own life to save another. Molly could tell that her mother had been crying and she was worried that Lynette might ship her back to Lubbock posthaste, to a place where no waves threatened to sweep her off the face of the earth. She waited for her mother to chastise her for risking her life but, instead, Lynette hugged her so hard that she thought her ribs might crack.

"All afternoon I tried to imagine what it would be like for you to live with your father and his new wife and her three big, blond *Swedish* children." She said it like it was something dirty, which Molly considered even more ironic considering how Swedes were generally thought to be so clean. "How could I even think about letting you go back to

Lubbock when I can't even imagine what I'm going to do without you for the week you're gone to Hawaii?"

Once again let's recap. My mother is no longer pissed off at me. I have a boyfriend—two, if you count Flea. I have friends. I'm good at something besides the saxophone. I have a six-pack for real ripples on my stomach. And I've been invited to five parties this weekend, which means I'm officially popular. And did I mention I'm a hero?

Contented, she posted her blog, this time for the entire world to see. She now had everything she wanted. The girl who had struggled to fit in, to find a place, who had lied her way to attention had been catapulted up the social food chain all the way to the A-list in less than five months. There was no doubt about it: It was good to be Molly.

"This is so like *The O.C.*, only better," AJ said as he scanned the backyard party at a mansion on the hill that had a breathtaking view of the entire South Bay.

Lounging around the pool were the beautiful people from Beach High, the jocks, the dance squad, the party girls, and a contingent from the ASB, including Andrea. Molly arrived with her entourage of surfers, whom she quickly ditched when Andrea waved her over. Unlike Andrea's party, there were no open kegs, kids were drinking but they were much more discrete.

"It's strictly BYOWB," Andrea commented, and then explained to Molly, "bring your own water bottle."

"Filled with vodka, right?"

"Molly, you surprise me. Would you like a sip from mine?" Andrea said, holding out her bottle of designer water.

Molly declined, and Andrea introduced her to her friends, treating Molly like she was a celebrity. All the girls had similar names, like Brittany (four of those) or Caitlin (six and counting), or Taylor (spelled three different ways), and almost all the girls had the same color hair, ranging from dark blond with streaked highlights to platinum, none of it totally natural. The guys stood in muscle-bound groups, talking boisterously, preening like male peacocks. As a local band began to play, Andrea pulled Molly aside, "So do you still like Kai, or are you going out with Flea, because that's what Riki told me."

Molly worried about sharing the details of her love life with Andrea. She hadn't completely trusted Andrea since the birthday party debacle, but she really needed advice. Besides, she couldn't resist talking about it now that she actually had a love life to share and a friend, albeit an imperfect one, to share it with.

"Kai and I are so together," Molly said, studying Andrea's face for a reaction. And seeing none, Molly felt comfortable enough to continue. "But the problem is, Flea thinks we have something going on, which is not true, but every time I try to talk to him about it, I freeze. It's like I can't confront him. And I don't know why."

"That is totally doable. If Flea feels like he dumped you, then he'll be fine with you seeing someone else."

"How do I make that happen?"

"You're at a party; there are guys. Flirt. Act, well, you know slutty. Flea wants a relationship," she said, making imaginary quotes with her fingers.

Molly scouted the party, looking for a candidate. Andrea suggested a hunky football player named Josh, who was splayed out on a lounger near the pool, describing how he single-handedly won the game against Redondo to a group of buddies who were so stoned, they didn't mind hearing his boring, self-serving, play-by-play account. When Molly protested that he looked like he was plastered, Andrea noted that being drunk was precisely the reason he was a perfect pick. "He'll do anything I ask him to."

And it was amazingly easy for Andrea to entice the inebriated football player to dance with Molly. After a quick word to the band to play a slow tune and even quicker introductions, Andrea left the couple alone on the patio. Molly worried that she wouldn't have anything to say, but she soon learned that conversation was totally unnecessary.

All he wanted to do was grope her while they danced. And she discovered in their sleazy embrace that she didn't have to act like a slut to be treated like one.

Unfortunately, Flea didn't see any of it. He disappeared inside the house with Andrea as soon as the dance began, unnoticed by Molly. But Kai watched from the grass, dazed and confused.

Josh hunched over Molly, stumbling. Afraid of his falling and her being crushed by a two hundred and forty-pound linebacker, Molly bailed from her original plan and tried to extract herself from his grasp. She wiggled out of his embrace and made excuses. But instead of letting her go, he cupped her butt and picked her up like a rag doll. She begged him to put her back down, but he pretended not to hear.

"Are you deaf as well as dumb?" Kai asked the linebacker as he tapped him on the shoulder. "Can't you see that she doesn't want to dance with you?"

He dropped her unceremoniously. Molly tried to smooth out the awkward situation. "I get nervous when my feet aren't touching the ground. I'm sorry about the dance, but please don't make this into a big deal, okay?"

Josh shrugged and ambled away, unconcerned. Molly was stunned. Even though she had asked him to not make a big deal of the situation, she certainly expected him to.

"Did you think he would fight me for you?" Kai asked when Molly expressed her chagrin.

"That's the way it would have gone down in Texas."

"Well, here, guys save it for the game," Kai said as they walked off the patio and into the beautifully landscaped yard. "Why were you dancing with him, anyway?"

"It was part of my plan to make Flea fall out of love with me."

"Well, it's not a very good plan. Because Flea isn't even around."

"Where did he go?" Molly wondered.

"Last time I saw him, he was in the game room having an animated discussion with Andrea on the hidden symbolism in *Pinky and the Brain*. Besides, haven't you learned by now that maybe honesty as a policy has a lot to recommend it?"

Even though she recognized that Kai had higher moral standards than she, Molly hated it when he *acted* morally superior. And she decided to test the waters, to see how high his standards were.

"You're right, Kai. We should be honest with each other. So why don't you start by telling me what really happened in Andrea's bedroom the night of her party?"

"Wow, that was random," Kai said, stopping.

"You said telling the truth was on your top-ten list of

things you liked about people; well, guess what? It's moving up on my list too."

"Okay, if you really want to know. Here's the deal. She's not your friend. Because friends don't go after guys you like."

"So something did happen with Andrea in her bedroom?"

"A little something, yeah. And that's all I'm going to say about it. Besides, technically you and I aren't even going out."

"Yeah, just like technically we weren't making out in the parking lot of the hospital either," Molly hissed.

They bantered back and forth, halfway locked in argument, testing the parameters of their undefined relationship. Having had enough of the evening, the party, and, frankly, Molly, Kai pressured her to leave with the rest of the Dawn Patrol, who were bored and feeling out of place. It was not their kind of party.

"Well, what if it's *my* kind of party?" asked Molly, who was having a good time and loving being the center of attention and hadn't bothered to make her old friends feel included.

"Why would you want to hang out with these people?" Kai asked.

"Because they like me," Molly said, trying not to think about how lame she sounded.

"Okay, we'll stay another hour, but then we've really got to go. We've got an early morning call, remember?"

Molly nodded. Because Surf Ed. had been cancelled all week due to the storm conditions, Duke, fully recovered, had suggested a surfing safari on Saturday. But after an hour more at the party, Molly was even less ready to go home. So her entourage left without her, and Molly spent the rest of the evening dancing with other popular girls. They were a wild bunch, most of them a little drunk, but they were fun. And they made her feel included, a part of something special and exclusive. She felt a little guilty about ignoring her surfing buddies, but she also knew they would get over it. And, besides, she told herself, she had a whole new set of friends, most of whom she couldn't identify by name. But so what? She'd get their names straight eventually. She'd figure it all out. She was on a roll.

EIGHTEEN

EARLY SATURDAY MORNING BEFORE SUN-RISE, THE DAWN PATROL CONGREGATED outside Duke's gear for the safari. Flea checked the surf conditions on his laptop to see where the good breaks were firing while the others strapped some of the boards to the top of Kai's wagon. AJ loaded his two custom-shaped sticks into the back of Duke's truck. As Molly tumbled down the steps of her trailer, still half asleep, Flea announced that they were predicting a south swell with head-high rollers at San Onofre, one of the premiere surf breaks in San Diego County, long considered the Waikiki of the California coastline.

"Why do we have to schlep all the way down the coast? Can't we find something closer?" Molly asked, having only gotten about three hours' sleep.

"She just doesn't get it," Buzz complained.

"That's because she's never been there," Duke said as

he stuck one of his oldest boards in the back of his truck. It was missing a fin and badly dinged; some of the foam had even torn away. AJ disapproved. "That looks like the first board my grandmother surfed on," he said, then added judgmentally, "after it had been run over by a car."

"This old board likes head-high, down-the-line surfing. It's perfect for relaxed, good-cruising waves," Duke said.

As they divided into cars, Flea volunteered that he and Molly would ride with Duke. Molly exchanged a look of longing with Kai as he refilled his water jug from the hose. She wanted to ride with him almost as much as she didn't want to ride to with Flea.

Sandwiched between Duke and Flea in the cab of the truck, she watched with regret in the rearview mirror as they pulled away, leaving Kai and the others far behind. In the short time it took to reach the Pacific Coast Highway, Flea tried to put his arm around her—twice. She shook him off, annoyed. But what annoyed her even more was during the first hour of the ride, Duke never brought up his near-drowning incident. He didn't even thank Molly for saving his life. And he managed to further irritate Molly by questioning her about her father's Hawaiian wedding.

"My mom thinks he's going through a midlife crisis. And I'd just as soon he go through it without me. So, can we talk about something else?" Molly asked.

"He's your father. You can't ignore him. Well, actually you can. But you might regret it."

"I don't know who's more annoying: You, Duke, or YOU," she said, screaming at Flea, who had casually slipped his hand across the back of the seat and down to her shoulder for about the tenth time. "Quit touching me," Molly hissed, and Flea retreated, confused. After all, just a week ago, she had said that she liked him.

They rode the rest of the way without speaking, which suited Duke, accommodated Molly, and aggravated Flea. He plugged into his iPod so he could escape their insufferable silence.

If Molly wondered why they had to drive an hour and a half to get to San Onofre, passing by a hundred miles of coastline with good surf, her questions were answered when she saw San O' for the first time, a magical fetch of coastline just north of Camp Pendleton. They walked down an undeveloped, chaparral-covered bluff, a testament to what all of California must have looked like a hundred years ago. They trudged across a stretch of sandy beach and claimed one of the unoccupied grass huts for their camp. AJ scanned the horizon as he unpacked his gear.

"Looks like some fast lefts firing at the Point," AJ said, noting the head-high southwest swell.

Locals divided San Onofre into three main breaks: the

Point, which often shut down in winter but was firing today. To the south was Old Man's, where the waves rolled off a padded reef and were mushier than melting ice cream. And finally there was Dogpatch, ideal for beginners who couldn't make the fifteen-minute paddle out to Old Man's.

"You guys go on. I'll take Molly out to Old Man's first and we'll work out way to the Point," Duke said.

Riki, AJ, Waldo, Buzz, Flea, and Kai suited up, stretching out the arms and legs of their wet suits, eager to join the lineup. Molly remained behind with Duke, who waxed his board methodically.

"What's going on with you and Flea?" Duke wondered.

"Nothing, and that's the problem, because he thinks something is," Molly said.

"What's going on with you and Kai?"

"Something, and that's the other problem," Molly said, sighing.

"Good golly, Miss Molly, who knew you'd turn into a femme fatale," Duke said, smiling.

"Shut. Up. One more comment like that and next time I will let you drown," Molly said, teasing.

"Good to know," Duke said.

As Duke waxed the rails of the board, she told him that a reporter from the local paper had called, expressing interest in doing a feature story about the rescue, telling it from three different perspectives: hers, Kai's, and Duke's. Flattered and eager for even more attention, this time from the press, no less, Molly assured the reporter that the three of them would be more than happy to be interviewed.

Duke shook his head. "I don't think that's such a good idea."

"Why not?"

"Let's just say that the press had never been kind to me. Call the reporter and tell him he can write a story about you and Kai but that I don't want to be interviewed."

Disappointed, Molly paddled out through the slow, lazy rollers behind Duke, joining the lineup where six older guys, two of them seriously overweight and one with his Labrador retriever on the board, were positioned and ready to rip.

"Now I know why they call it Old Man's," Molly commented as she and Duke sat hunched over their boards waiting for the next languid swell to roll their way.

"Well, California surf culture isn't all *Baywatch* babes," Duke said, just as the first in the lineup, a white-haired gent, took off at what looked to be the right time but pulled out, missing the wave altogether. Duke explained the intricacies of catching a wave at San O'.

"What you have to understand about San Onofre is that the waves are indecisive. They like to crest, back off, and crest again before they finally break. They say you can die from old age waiting for that 'one last wave of the day,' but that's not the point at San O'."

"And what is the point at San O'?" Molly asked.

"You tell me when the day is over," Duke said with Zenlike serenity.

Duke and Molly drifted away from the others, watching as the dog owner took off down the face of a lazy roller, his Labrador perched on the nose of the board like the bowsprit on a boat. Following Duke's advice, Molly caught half a dozen of rides, but Duke stayed in the lineup, unwilling to waste energy on anything less than perfection. The first wave he caught, he executed a flawless cutback, turning back toward the breaking part of the wave. Molly watched in awe of how masterfully Duke maneuvered his old board. He made it perform like a brand-new Spyder.

"Not bad," Molly quipped as Duke rejoined her in the lineup.

They rolled with the swells in comfortable silence for a long time before Duke finally said, "I always thought when it was my time to go, I would die in the water."

"Waldo thinks you did die in the water. Seriously. He believes you were resurrected. That's his theory, anyway."

"What's your theory?"

"I don't have one. I've been waiting for you to tell me

what happened. If you won't talk to a reporter, then talk to me. Because I want to know why you went out. And what happened. And how you got into trouble."

"That's a lot of questions."

"Okay, let's start with one. Why weren't you wearing a wet suit?"

"I didn't bother with a wet suit because all I wanted was one good ride in a big winter storm. And even though I make all of you swear to never go out by yourself, I do it all the time. I got through the impact zone easily, but the chop was more intense than I'd first thought. And out where they were breaking were big gobs of kelp that had broken free, some of them so large that they went down four feet below the surface. Which is how I got into trouble. My leash got tangled up in a ball of kelp, throwing my board perpendicular to the set. I dove under to untangle it and got caught in a current. I became disoriented. I thought I was headed for the surface, but hit the bottom. And for some reason, I inhaled salt water instead of exhaling breath. I was halfway drowned by the time I made it to the top and grabbed my board. I couldn't even draw breath. So I hung on to my board until I couldn't any longer. And then I just slipped away. It was easy."

Something about the way he said it—even the choice of the word "easy"—made Molly very uncomfortable. He sensed her own unease and tried to explain.

"The point is, I'm not afraid to die. I've lived a lot longer than I thought I would."

"You're not that old. You're in a lot better shape than he is," Molly said, gesturing to a balding geezer in the lineup who looked like he was wearing an inner tube of whale blubber inside his wet suit.

"I used to laugh at guys who missed the morning break because they were working hard to get ahead in their careers. I didn't have to worry about that because I didn't think I'd make it to thirty, much less retirement. I seriously believed that I would die before I had to figure out what to do with myself in any real way. And then one day, you wake up and you're middle-aged, with either too much time on your hands or not enough, depending on the day and your perspective."

Again, Molly pestered Duke to talk to the reporter. "Think how awesome it would be to have our picture in the paper and everything. Look, I'm afraid if you won't do the interview, he won't do the story. So you see, you have to say yes."

But again, Duke refused, saying that the only way he could work up the nerve to talk to another reporter would be to have a drink, and if he had a drink, then he would tell the reporter the whole story, one that he preferred not to share.

"What is the whole story?" Molly asked, wondering what he could have possibly left out.

"I didn't really want to be saved," Duke said simply.

"I don't understand."

"It would have been okay if you had just let me go."

She didn't know how to respond or even how to process what she had just heard. How do you make sense of having risked your own life to save someone only to discover that the person you rescued didn't want to be saved? But before she could question him further—as if she could have figured out what to ask—they were interrupted by the appearance of something majestic.

"Look, Molly," Duke whispered, pointing to the north.

"Oh. My. God," Molly said, breathless.

Half a mile off shore, a giant fluke rose out of the ocean, slapping the water as a California Gray whale breached and then dove back down to feed. Two more whales surfaced, swimming very close to each other, perhaps drafting on the first whale Duke first spotted. The California Grays traveled down the coast every winter, leaving their feeding grounds in the Bering Sea to return to the calving lagoons of Baja, a five-thousand-mile journey. As the two disappeared, the first whale resurfaced to breathe. Its blow shot straight into the air and miraculously turned into a rainbow of mist in the light, an arced prism of colors that disappeared so fast, Molly wondered if she actually saw a rainbow made from a whale's blow or if she had made it up. She turned to Duke with a "Did you see what I just saw?" expression on her face. A look of understanding passed between them, referencing an earlier conversation about how sometimes the best part of surfing is sitting out on the board, surging with the swells, and letting life unfold.

An hour after they spotted the California Grays, they moved to the Point and joined the others, where they surfed away the afternoon. Molly had a lot more wipe-outs than usual that day, probably because there were some six-foot sets that were hard to time. But she managed a nice floater in the late afternoon, riding on top of the wave, and she should have stopped then, calling it a day. Instead, she paddled back into the lineup. As the sun began its descent, Molly cut along the face of a wave and looked out toward the ocean, remembering the pod of whales she had seen earlier and wondering if there were more of those graceful creatures beyond the breakers. She stared into the face of the wave and the lip broke right into her own face, white water shooting straight up her nose. She cut out of the ride and rolled back to shore, coughing up seawater as she lugged her board onto the shore. Done for the day, she stripped out of her wet suit and changed from her bikini into dry clothes in one of the public bathrooms.

When she emerged, the sun was just beginning to dip into the water, painting swirls of orangey red with the last strokes of daylight. It was time to head home, but Duke and Kai stayed in the lineup, waiting for one last taste of magic. And even though she was eager to return to her beach and the three parties that beckoned, Molly understood that obsessive need to catch that one last wave. Many a surfer had set on his board past darkness long after he should have wrapped it up, unable to break free of the spell of the last ride. It was as illogical as it was strong, that feeling that the opportunity might never present itself again.

A dark shadow appeared on the horizon, a wall of approaching foam. And like an answered prayer, a rogue wave peaked, eight feet at least, a left-over from the last week's winter storms. It was long and hollow, with a wide open end on the shoulder. Kai pulled out of the ride and nodded to his mentor to go for it. Duke took off and paddled like hell. He came from behind the peak, pulled into the barrel, and maneuvered into a position where the wave curled over him, forming a tube. He disappeared inside it as deeply as possible. The wall of water stretched out before him endlessly, bright blue at the end.

On the shore, a small crowd had gathered to watch Duke as he commandeered the best wave of the day and rode it all the way in. Getting barreled was the holy grail of surfing. And to see Duke do it was to witness a thing of beauty. When he reached the white water, he stepped off the board in one easy movement, the transition from water to land seamless, graceful. Duke waded through the white-water soup toward Molly and the others.

"So how was it, brah?" Flea asked.

Duke grinned from hell to breakfast. "That is as close as I'll ever come to looking into the face of God."

Buzz and Waldo nodded in solemn agreement.

"What do you think of my grandmother board now, AJ?" Duke asked.

"I may have misjudged," AJ said evenly.

"You can't buy karma, AJ, and this board's dripping with it," Duke said, smiling. He left them to say hello to a whole tribe of surfers, many of whom he knew personally, who were swilling beer and sharing stories under one of the grassy huts. Best wave ever surfed and the ones that were missed. The most body-whomping break or bone-crunching wipeout. If there were one thing surfers were never short of, it was stories.

Away from the others, Kai tossed Molly his sweatshirt as they huddled around a small bonfire built from driftwood on the beach.

"Thanks. I always forget how cold it gets when the sun goes down," Molly said.

"If you're going to be a California girl, you have to learn to always carry a sweatshirt," Kai said.

"'If' being the operative word here," Molly said.

He could tell she was upset and he asked her if something else had happened with Flea. She shrugged. Flea was a problem, but he was not *the* problem. High school drama took a backseat to what troubled her now, a subject she didn't even know how to broach. Off and on all day long, she mulled over what Duke had said to her. Did his confession require a response on her part? Should she talk to someone? Should she insist that he get help? Should he be on a suicide watch? Having saved his life, was she now responsible for it?

"If you think someone's in trouble but know that they want you to leave them alone, should you try to get them help or should you respect their wishes and back off?"

"Who is that someone in trouble?"

"Duke."

Kai looked across the beach at Duke holding court with his surfing buddies, laughing and sharing stories. He did not look like a man in trouble. He looked like a man having a good time. A very good time.

"What are you talking about? He's great. Cheerful, even."

"He went out into the ocean on Tuesday hoping to die."

"Did he say that?"

"Not in those words, but . . ."

Kai thought she was wrong. Duke would never try to kill himself; he was not that kind of guy.

"Your problem, Molly is that you're too impulsive. You're always rushing into things without thinking. We should have waited for the guard before going in. We could have died trying to help. So maybe you should try waiting, giving it some thought, before you go in and mess something up that maybe you don't understand."

"Sometimes, Kai, you really piss me off," she said, "and other times, you just make me mad."

NINETEEN

IN THE TWO WEEKS THAT FOLLOWED THE TRIP TO SAN ONOFRE, MOLLY BEGAN TO believe that she had completely misconstrued her earlier conversation with Duke. Maybe Kai had been right after all. Because Duke did seem cheerful, energetic, revived from his near-brush with death. And as Waldo continuously pointed out, "Resurrected. The man has a whole new perspective."

And as that larger-than-life drama subsided, the high school soap opera grew, taking up emotional space. Molly's brush with instant popularity waned because she was at heart not a party girl. Her fifteen minutes of fame fizzled in about fourteen. The invitations stopped before she could even correctly identify a Caitlin from a Brittany. And while she didn't miss any of those particular individuals, she did miss the attention. Even Andrea dropped her, entrenched in other activities and obligations, which suited Molly just fine. Because Molly had come to realize that even though

Andrea gave great parties and was well known and respected by her peers, she was seriously lacking one element necessary to qualify her for a contender in the best-friend category: She could not be trusted. And as much as Molly hated to admit it, because there were tremendous benefits to having a rich, popular friend, having a friend you couldn't trust was worse than having no friend at all.

Her dance card emptied, Molly started hanging with the surfing crowd exclusively, but the easy camaraderie that had once existed between them had changed as well. There was an unspoken tension in the air that she attributed to the problem with Flea. Despite her being mean and dismissive to him, he continued to treat her like his girlfriend in front of the others, which added an odd dynamic to the group, and threatened the tenuous balance of personalities in the Dawn Patrol.

"Hey, can you drop Molly and me off at the Quickie-Mart? We're going to grab a soda and go down to the beach for a little alone-time," Flea told Kai as they were cruising their beach town on a Friday evening, the entire Dawn Patrol crammed into the Volvo wagon.

Kai pulled into the parking lot and Flea was the first to bail. Resolved, Molly touched Kai's shoulder and said, "Ten minutes is all we need."

Molly waited for Flea to buy a super-size soda and then

suggested they walk through the Hermosa neighborhood instead of going to the beach. A quarter moon burnished orange on midnight blue waters was way too romantic a setting for the conversation she needed to have with Flea. They turned down a sleepy residential street.

"You have to quit acting like we're going out. Look, I like you, but I don't like you in that way," Molly said. "And I'm sorry, because I wish I did."

Flea was not only devastated, he just didn't get it. "So what's the deal? Am I not your type? Is that it?"

"Look at us. We're exactly the same type. We could be twins."

"So are you into somebody else? Is that what's going on?"

She cast her eyes down to the pavement, not wanting to give herself away.

"Who? No, let me guess. Kai."

Molly was surprised; she didn't think it was that apparent. "How did you know?"

"I didn't. I was being purposefully ironic. God, this is going to be awkward."

Molly stopped and looked at Flea and for just an instant, she wished he had been the one to rescue her in the rip.

"The truth is, if I hadn't fallen for him, I'd be totally into you. And sometimes I wish it had worked out that way because I think it would be easier to be with you than it is to be with him. You're a really great guy."

She waited for his reaction, but he said nothing. They walked in silence past a three-story Tudor mansion and a bleached-wood four-plex. They passed two more remodels before he finally stopped to ask, "So do you think you could hook me up with Andrea?"

She slugged him on the shoulder. "Could you please at least act upset for about five minutes before you shout, 'Next,' and move on to your next crush?"

He got suddenly serious. "Just so you know, Molly, you weren't a crush."

Touched by his admission, which revealed a depth of feeling she hadn't earned, expected, or appreciated nearly enough, she leaned over and kissed him lightly on the cheek just as Kai pulled up beside them, honking.

"See, I told you they were an item," Riki said to AJ as Molly and Flea climbed into the backseat.

"Actually, no," Flea said. "We broke up."

"Good. Now can we go back to normal again?" AJ asked hopefully.

But they would never go back. Certainly not to normal. And never to the way it had been before. The evening would unfurl in a way none of them could have predicted. And all of their lives were about to be changed forever.

• • •

"Hey, that's four—maybe even five sirens. Let's see what's up," Kai said, turning onto Pier Avenue, glad for a diversion, even if it was ambulance chasing.

"I vote no. Ever since we got arrested, I'm not as into other people's pain," Buzz said.

"Oh, come on, there's nothing else to do," Riki insisted.

Deciding to go for it, Kai whipped the wheel into a fast left on Bay View. Flea's jumbo, super-size soda from the Quickie-Mart spilled, soaking AJ's brand-new Quicksilver cargo pants and littering the floor with dozens of small, square ice cubes. In retaliation, AJ picked up a handful of ice, chucked some of it at Kai for turning too fast, clobbered Flea for buying super-size to begin with and stuck ice down the back of Riki's blouse on general principles. The icy gauntlet thrown down, a full-fledged fight erupted, ice flying everywhere. Kai pulled over to regroup. Riding shotgun, Riki rolled down the window and pointed at what appeared to be a searchlight at the top of the bluff.

"Shut up and listen," she commanded the group. The sound of an ambulance Klaxon whining drifted toward them, coming from the same direction as the light. Kai turned and started up the hill.

Kai slowed as they neared a small beach cottage surrounded by five police cars; the red spinning lights on top of the cars reflected off the front bay window. An ambulance was just pulling away as they arrived. Kai parked, and they bailed from the car, on a midnight adventure with half a dozen other lookie-loo neighbors who had wandered out of the houses to see what was going on. They inched toward the police tape that cordoned off the entire front yard and part of the street. Being the smallest, Molly elbowed her way to the front to get a good look.

In the front yard crashed into a tree was a mangled red Tacoma truck. One of the cop's flashlights flashed through the darkness, tracking across the truck's back bumper and illuminating the peeling sticker: EDDIE WOULD DO IT. She and Kai saw the sign at exactly the same moment. And they knew. It was Duke's truck.

Kai and Molly crawled under the police tape, leaving their friends behind. Squabbling among themselves over who actually had started the ice fight, they were oblivious to their personal connection to the crash.

Two steps into the yard, Kai and Molly were stopped by one of the cops, who urged them to get back behind the caution tape. But Molly refused. "Look, we know the owner of that truck," she said.

Thinking that they might be of some assistance to the investigation, the cop led them across the lawn to Officer Price, who was finishing up a call to the precinct.

"It would be him," Molly whispered to Kai as they approached the burly cop, Duke's nemesis.

Tonight, Price seemed more subdued than he had been when Molly had first met him, as if the venom in his poisonous tone had been extracted. In a calm, monotone voice, he explained that Duke's truck had crossed the southbound lane, crashed through the three-foot-high picket fence, and ended up in the yard. The impact with the tree stopped it; otherwise, it would have kept on going into the house. He spoke about Duke's truck as if there were no driver involved. Duke's truck did this. Duke's truck did that. They pressed for information about their friend.

"When we arrived on the scene, we found Duke lying facedown in the middle of the street. For whatever reason, he had crawled out of the passenger side of the truck and started out, maybe to get help, maybe he thought the vehicle would catch fire, but he wandered into the middle of the road and collapsed."

"Is he okay?" Kai asked.

"He sustained some major head injuries," Officer Price said, looking away. Clearly more comfortable talking about the accident than the victim, he continued, "There were no skid marks on the road, and it didn't appear excessive speed was involved. Of course, we'll check the truck to see if there were any mechanical difficulties."

Molly dug her nails into her sides in an effort to replace the feeling of nothingness that overwhelmed her with something, anything, even pure physical pain. "Do you think he did it on purpose?" she asked.

Officer Price leveled his gaze at Molly. "Is there something you want to tell me?"

"Do you think it was intentional?"

"Well, there's no way of knowing that. Not yet, anyway. But if you know something that would indicate this was a suicide attempt, then you have a legal obligation to tell us," Officer Price said, his gruffness returning.

"Molly gets carried away. She's from Texas," Kai said, as if that explained it.

Evidently, geography counted in Officer's Price's prejudicial eyes. Being from Texas could explain lots of things, including impetuousness. He waved them on brusquely, allowing them to leave.

Kai gently chastised Molly as they made their way back to the group on the other side of the caution tape. "Don't get ahead of yourself, okay? We shouldn't say anything to the cops until after we talk to Duke."

The Dawn Patrol rushed across the beautifully manicured grounds and into the front doors of Torrance Memorial, descending on the front desk en masse.

"We want some information about one of your patients, Duke Updike. He was brought here by ambulance," Flea said.

The officious, pleasant-speaking receptionist with a round face and long ponytail asked how to spell his last name and then checked her computer. "Are you sure he was brought to this hospital?" she asked. "Because he's not in the system. I have no record of his being admitted."

"He was in a car accident in Hermosa. The cops said they were bringing him here," Kai insisted.

"Well, let me see what I can find out for you." While she called down to the emergency room to get more information, AJ and Waldo pooled their resources and emptied the snack machines in the front foyer, building a supply of fortifications, assuming that it might be a while before they could actually see Duke.

The round receptionist gently put the phone back into the cradle and stood. She smiled weakly, and her voice quivered as she asked them to follow her. She led them down a long, brightly lit corridor and through the double doors to the ER and stuck them in a small triage room.

"Is Duke in surgery?" Kai asked.

"Someone will be here in a minute to answer all your questions. It won't be long," she said before disappearing.

"Long," in hospital terms is always relative. There were

seven of them and only one chair in the small room, which Riki immediately claimed. Kai and Molly perched on the examining table, leaving AJ, Flea, Buzz, and Waldo to fend for themselves. They slumped to the floor. AJ emptied his pockets of the snacks from the vending machines. He ripped them open, one by one, took a bite, and then passed the bag to the next person in the circle, who took a handful and passed it on: cheese puffs followed by trail mix, followed by bite-size cookies, followed by peanuts and so on. After twenty minutes, along with the seven friends huddled in the crowded cubicle were fourteen crumpled junk food wrappers and still no word from the hospital authorities.

It was almost an hour before a young ER doctor came in the room accompanied by Archie, who had been called since he was listed as Duke's emergency contact from their last hospital sojourn. Archie's hair was tousled and his eyes bloodshot, like he'd been drinking or crying. He introduced them to the young doctor, who, in contrast to Archie, was meticulously groomed. The two men exchanged a worried glance before the doctor began. Before he even opened his mouth to speak, Molly knew that whatever he had to say, it was not good news.

Outside and mere miles away, the quarter moon shone on the silvery sea, casting ribbons of shiny streaks across the steely gray surface, like cracks in an antique mirror.

Back in the hospital triage cubicle, the young intern carefully chose his words, trying to translate the unthinkable into the manageable. But Molly interrupted, reeling with rage, disbelief, shock. She demanded to see Duke. Archie told her in no uncertain terms that she could not, that he would not allow it. He told her that Duke would not want her to see him like that; it was not the way he would want to be remembered, his head gashed open, his face slashed, his body mangled. The doctor continued; he told the group in very cold, clinical terms that Duke had never made it to surgery. He was DOA. The doctor's gaze drifted to the floor so he didn't have to look any of them in the eye. It was then that Molly heard this terrible sound, like something she had never heard before. A sound that could only be described as the pitiful wail of an unearthly creature, a cry out of darkness, maybe from the underworld itself, like the horrible shriek from a soul on its last pass through the familiar. It seemed to last forever. It was only when it stopped that she realized what it was. It was her, the sound of her own screams.

At Molly's request, Kai drove by the crash site on their way home. He pulled over and parked. She got out of the car, stepped over the shattered fence, and haltingly walked across the front yard so that she could get a closer look at the tree, the one that had ended Duke's life. She had remembered it as having a large trunk and menacing, over-hanging branches. But with the truck towed and the cars gone, she now had a clear view and what she found on closer inspection surprised her. The tree was neither large nor menacing; it was a melaleuca, a slender sapling. She touched the unusual bark, which looked like Japanese paper that had been peeled away, revealing layers of beauty. Molly wondered how anything so beautiful and so benign could have taken a life.

"It all feels pointless. Nothing we did mattered," Molly said, stripping down to her T-shirt and climbing under the blankets in her mother's bed.

Having promised to stay with her until she fell asleep, Kai crawled in the bed beside her. He wrapped around Molly like a spoon and held her as she sobbed into the pillow. Her staggering sense of guilt mirrored his own, yet unspoken. Without knowing why, he slipped on the burden of responsibility like an old, comfortable shirt. And his tears too began to flow.

She closed her eyes, convinced that all of them had somehow failed Duke, she especially. She cried for half an hour solid, her body racked with sobs. Exhausted, she fell sound asleep on a pillow wet from their tears. Kai left her and tiptoed into the living room. He put the television on low and settled into the sofa. In the early morning hours, he too drifted off into a sleep punctuated and disturbed by network reruns.

When Molly's mother returned from work at sunrise, she saw Kai's wagon parked out front. Upset, she flew into the house only to find Kai awake and waiting for her, Molly still sound sleep in her mother's bed. Even before he could say one word, she knew that something terrible had happened because the look on Kai's face was all too familiar. She knew that look; she had owned it. She saw in his eyes, red from crying, the pain of someone who had suffered a loss so big that the world would never be the same.

Miz Boyer was on her second cup of coffee when Lynette walked Kai to his car. She hugged him and thanked him for taking care of Molly. As Kai pulled out of the park, Miz Boyer peered at Lynette over the top of her glasses. "He was here all night, you know," she said to Lynette, who this time dismissed her catty gossip-mongering.

As Kai's wagon rolled over the last speed bump and pulled out of the park, Lynette explained to Miz Boyer what had happened the night before, how Duke had died in a car accident. Miz Boyer carefully set her coffee cup down on the wide porch railing. Shocked, she was unable to process the simple fact of his death. She crossed her arms and cradled her chin in her hand. Puzzled, she shook her head, chewing on the bad news and repeating to herself over and over again, "That doesn't sound right. It just doesn't sound right, does it?"

Inside the trailer, Molly slept. On and off for three whole days that blurred into night. She had no sense of time. She didn't shower. She barely ate. Her mother didn't make her go to school; she thought it best to let her daughter's grief run its course. Her surfing buddies called every day, but she refused to talk to them. Instead Molly, locked away in her room, made secret phone calls to Texas. She talked to her father, who listened to her cry. And she called Katie, who told her how much she missed her and how great everything was at school. Katie reached out across the miles and urged Molly to come home, back to Lubbock, certain that she would feel better in a place where people really understood her.

On the fourth day, Molly emerged from her bedroom to accompany Kai to the police station to see the accident report. As they walked the block and a half from the trailer park to the police station, Molly made new deals with God, praying that inside the old brick building they would find new insight, answers that would enable Molly to move past her anger. If she knew what had really happened on that night, it might make it easier to accept Duke's death. Kai pretended that he was going along as moral support for Molly, but the truth was, he had to go for himself. He needed answers as badly as she did.

They were shuffled into a cubicle, where Officer Price opened a very thin folder and began.

"We did a toxicity report and Duke had not been drinking, which was odd because it was, after all, a Friday night," Officer Price said.

Right from the get-go, Molly did not care for his disrespectful tone. Price continued, saying that the absence of skid marks was suspicious, indicating possible intent. But they had found no note or any other evidence to support the suicide theory. And although there was no way of knowing with any certainty what had happened to Duke that night, his death had been ruled an accident. Price shut the thin folder with a "case closed" finality.

"Did you run the tests to see if there had been some kind of mechanical failure with the truck?" Molly asked.

"What would be the point?" Price replied.

"I don't mean to be disrespectful, but it doesn't seem to me that you tried very hard to discover what happened, how he died."

In Molly's opinion, the size of the folder reflected a scarcity of effort.

"Since we could rule out homicide and since only one person was involved in the accident and that person had expired with no insurance policies at stake or lawsuits pending, I don't think it matters one way or the other," Price said.

"Well, it matters to us. And frankly, you make me so mad, I could just—"

She paused dramatically. Kai braced himself for the inevitable.

"Spit!" Molly said, finishing her thought.

But, thankfully, she didn't.

Molly and Kai left the police station and crossed the street. Kai paused when they reached the iron archway leading to the trailer park, taking her hand. "You know, you are really beautiful when you're angry."

"That is so unfortunate. Because I'm totally tired of being mad," she said.

Exhausted, she collapsed into his arms, and they held each other for a long time, each seeking a kind of cleansing comfort that their needy embrace failed to provide.

TWENTY

COOL SANTA ANA WINDS BLEW THROUGH
SOUTHERN CALIFORNIA AND BUFFETED
the sand south of the pier, turning the beach at Eighth
Street into a windswept Sahara. Chilly gusts of sand-
speckled wind stung their eyes as the Dawn Patrol gathered for Surf Ed. Molly arrived a little later than everyone
else, but no one was in the water yet. Without Duke, it
seemed awkward, strange. They parked their boards and
sat on the sand.

"So is there going to be a funeral or something?" Waldo
asked.

"We should ask Archie. He'd know," AJ offered.

Archie had been placed in charge of Surf Ed. until they
could find a permanent replacement for Duke. Archie told
the surfers that Duke's sister had given permission as next
of kin to have Duke's body cremated, but since they had
been estranged for years, she told the funeral home to give

his ashes to one of his surfer buddies. "So it's up to us. I'm calling around to see what we want to do."

Archie was called away, and the group was left to their own thoughts.

"You know there could be issues with a burial, because it might have been a—" Flea stopped, unable to even say the word "suicide" out loud. "I talked to my rabbi and he said that there were deep spiritual consequences for a person who takes their own life, and that there's a debate if you can even sit shiva."

"Which isn't really a problem," Molly remarked angrily, "since Duke wasn't Jewish."

Molly picked up her board—his board—and took it down to the water's edge, hoping that the water would help soothe her troubled soul. But she couldn't make it past the first set of breakers. Being in the ocean only magnified her sense of loss. She began sobbing; the pain ripping through her as fresh as it had been the day he died. She turned her board around and headed back in without even trying to catch a wave. She waded through the white water and turned to watch the others, to see how they fared. From her vantage point at the shoreline, it looked like any other ordinary day in Surf Ed. Twenty kids watched from the lineup as Waldo and AJ surfed a three-footer in tandem. It seemed to Molly that these California born and bred were dealing with their loss far better than she was. As she looked out over the turquoise waters, the wind whipping through her hair, she considered that perhaps Katie had been right.

She needed to find her roots. To return to a place where she would be safe. A place where it wouldn't hurt so much. She needed to go home to Texas.

Molly didn't go to school that day. Or the following. At the end of the week, Andrea stopped by the trailer after school, bringing Molly her homework assignments, a box of chocolate chip cookies, messages and notes from the jazz band, one of which was taped to a Ding Dong cupcake. Andrea had no idea how to ask Molly about what happened or how she was feeling. In Andrea's opinion, death was just too awkward a subject to talk about. So she directed the conversation into a safer, more familiar topic: herself. After rambling on about parties and projects, she finally broached a subject she considered to be of major importance.

"I have a confession to make. I tried to kiss Kai at my party and feel terrible about it."

"If you want to stop feeling guilty, then do penance or feed bread to the fishes, but don't ask me to forgive you."

"If it makes you feel any better, he didn't kiss me back."

"Which doesn't change what you did. Bottom line is I

don't even want to have this conversation. It doesn't matter anymore."

"Yes, it does. You're my friend, Molly. Probably my best friend."

"Well, that is beyond sad. If you want a real best friend, than you must learn to be a better one. But it'll have to be with somebody else. Because I'm just passing through."

That evening, Molly surfaced from her room and found her mom reading the morning paper at the evening meal, yet one more piece of evidence of a world turned up side down.

"I've decided to move back to Texas. Dad says it's okay," Molly announced.

Lynette carefully put down her glass; her hand trembled. "I was crazy to have even suggested it in the first place, but there is no way I'm going to let you go back to Texas and live with *that* woman."

"If you hadn't left Dad, he wouldn't be involved with *that* woman."

"That's not true," Lynette protested.

"Yes, it is!" she insisted.

Lynette's resolve to shield her daughter had worn thin and she was just plain tired of protecting a man who had betrayed her. She told Molly that there had been signs he had been seeing someone for some time, but she ignored them, holding on to false hope that she was imagining his affair. Molly's pressed for the details, wanting to know what had made her mother snap. Why did she leave him all of sudden, without warning?

"What do you want from me, Molly? Do you want me to tell you how I found a box, not a package, but an entire Costco-size box of condoms in the trunk of his car? Is that what you want to hear?"

Molly stepped into the shower stall, stared at the water marks on the ceiling, and let the warm water wash away the memory of her mother's revelation. For months, Molly had pressured her mother for an explanation as to why she had left her father. And now she had it. Knowing why something happened did not always result in making it better or easier. Sometimes it was just TMI—too much information.

Kai gave Molly the space he thought she needed, but when she stopped replying even to his text messages, he dropped by after school and knocked on her door repeatedly until she opened it. Molly was wearing an oversize T-shirt and Ugg boots; her hair was tangled. He was accustomed to seeing Molly disheveled and thrown together, but he had never seen her look like that.

"When are you coming back to school?"

"It doesn't matter if I go or not. I'm transferring out at the end of the quarter."

If the news rattled him, he didn't show it. He shuffled and then added, "They're releasing your sea lion today. I thought you might want to be there to see it."

"Thanks, but I don't feel like going anywhere, especially not to the ocean," Molly said, closing the door, but Kai stuck his foot in the door frame, preventing her from shutting him and the rest of the world out.

"I don't care what you *feel* like. This afternoon, you're going to get dressed and go with me to San Pedro. And if you want to shower, I'll wait."

Kai and Molly met Archie at the Marine Center. They were releasing two sea lions that day; the first was the older female Molly rescued who had survived a septic infection from the wounds on her neck. She had flourished in the center, gained weight, and was back up to her 250 pounds. The other was an abandoned sea pup who had spent ten months in the center. To facilitate his socialization, he was placed with the older sea lion and they had formed an immediate bond. In fact, the center decided to hold the female's release for a couple of weeks until after the pup had mastered how to dive and catch fish on his own so that they could be released together.

As they waited at the truck for the volunteers to coerce the wild sea lions into large plastic cages used as airplane carriers for dogs, Archie discussed the funeral arrangements for Duke. Molly, uncharacteristically quiet, listened as the other two made plans for a service on the water, a memorial paddle-out. She, however, had no interest in attending a funeral for her mentor, not until she had some answers, some definite proof that his death had been an accident and not intentional.

"This is not right. You should be worrying about the prom or homecoming or whatever. Not trying to make sense of one man's reckless journey," Archie said.

"Just so you know, trying to make sense of that other stuff sucks too," Molly quipped.

"You knew him best, Archie. What do you think happened?" Kai asked.

Uncertain, Archie plunged ahead into territory he felt best left uncharted. "Look, I'm not sure I have all the answers you want, but I do know that Duke had thought about suicide from time to time."

Molly's anger, which had subsided in the last week, returned full blown, like a relapse of the flu. "How could he be so selfish? How could he go to our beach first thing in the morning with that singular purpose in mind? He had to have known that we would be the ones to find him."

"Suicide is the ultimate act of selfishness," Archie said.

"Why did he do it? What was so terrible that he felt like he had to check out? I want to understand. I really do," she said.

"Like I said, I don't know anything for sure. But Duke was sick. He'd been having stomach problems for a few months now."

"What was wrong?" Kai asked, growing nervous.

"I don't know. I'm not even sure if he'd gone to the doctor. You know how he was. But I do know he was scared, not of dying, but of getting weak and wasting away. And he talked about suicide from time to time as a viable alternative if things got bad."

"Was he worried that he had cancer?" Kai asked, choking back tears.

Kai revealed that during his mother's own battle with cancer, he had shared with Duke how much trouble she'd had tolerating the chemo, how she had jokingly complained that if the disease didn't kill her, the treatment might. And now he worried that he might have unintentionally discouraged Duke from getting help when he needed it.

"Don't even go there. You are not responsible. God, you're even worse than me," Molly said.

But neither her admonition nor Archie's insistence that he was blameless could keep Kai from feeling guilty. As the volunteers loaded the cages in the back of the truck, Archie made one more attempt to unburden the two of them—Molly from her anger, and Kai from his guilt.

"The last time Duke and I got together was a week before he died, and he seemed like his old self. We had a great time, telling our stories, giving each other a hard time. He didn't mention a word about checking out. So for what's it worth, here's my version of his story. On that January morning, he walked down to the water with his board, with every intention of riding his last wave. He gave himself up to the ocean, like a human sacrifice. That's what I believe. But you guys screwed it up. You went in balls out and saved him. But sometime after that, he had an epiphany. I think he changed his mind. I think instead of giving up, he dug in. The Duke I saw during the last two weeks of his life was a man who had decided on life. So, in my opinion, what happened—the accident—was just that. It was an accident."

It took the three of them and two trips to carry the heavy cages with the sea lions from the parking lot down to an isolated stretch of beach with no one in sight to interfere with the sea lions' path to freedom. Archie opened the cages and stepped back. The pup stuck his head out first tentatively, sniffing the air like a dog. He took a few cautious steps out of the cage, and the older female followed. She turned back to Molly with a bewildered look on her face. Molly could see the scars from the wound encircling her neck, what was once a necklace of pain was now a faint tattoo, a permanent reminder of her own brush with death. The sea lion arched her back and faced the ocean, letting the onshore breeze caress her skin with memories of the place where she belonged. Hearing the call of the sea, she barked loudly and led the charge across the sand followed by the pup, sliding over the wet hard-pack and into the water, swimming away from the shore as three pelicans flew overhead. She never once looked back.

Archie loaded the empty cages into the back of his truck, giving Kai and Molly a moment alone on the shore. They watched the three large pelicans swoop and dive for fish.

"We should have let him die in the water," she said. "It's what he wanted."

"Even if we had known that, I don't think it would have changed what we did."

"What troubles me most is that I don't think he died an easy death," she said, choking back tears.

"Don't think about that."

"I don't know how to stop."

"You keep saying that nothing we did made a difference. Well, remember Duke at San O' when he dropped

inside the tube? If it hadn't been for you, he never would have caught that ride. And even if the only thing you ever gave him was that one more good day on the water, doesn't that count for something?" He put his arm on her shoulder, and she leaned her head against his chest.

"I don't want you to move back to Texas," he said finally. "The only way we can get through this is together."

"I know it's hard for you to understand why I have to go, because you belong here. But right now I need to be in a place that feels like home."

And there on the sand, in the warm winter sun, she kissed him good-bye. There were a lot of things she would miss about California, and on top of that list was kissing Kai.

At the first light of a fogbound California morning, five hundred surfers, all clad in white memorial T-shirts gathered at their pier, staring out at the gray expanse of Pacific. For the Dawn Patrol, it was their first memorial paddle-out. They lingered on the pier, wondering where Molly was and if she would come. As they waited, they watched with amazement as more and more people showed up to honor Duke. Buzz pointed out dozens of surfing greats. And among those legends on the water were also men and women who made a living on the water. AJ noted true movers and shakers who designed boards and made surfing gear. There were also former students, six years' worth of Surf Ed. classes and locals—attorneys, shop owners, waiters—all who had shared beers, waves, and stories with their fallen brother. In groups small and large, they strolled down to the sandy beach and entered the surf to make their way out past the four-foot breakers to the calm, deep waters past the reef.

Molly stayed home, tucked away inside her bedroom. Open suitcases littered the floor, bags half packed. In less than a week she would leave for Texas. Laptop open on her bed, she composed her last entry from California.

I decided not to go to Duke's memorial. I didn't see any point in it. Because memorials aren't for the people who have passed; they're for the living. And I didn't think going to his would make me feel any better. Besides, it seemed hypocritical to honor somebody when I was still mad at him for leaving me.

I had always believed that if I only knew why people did what they did—why my mom left my father or why Duke tried to kill himself—I would be able to forgive them for hurting me. But truth doesn't set you free from anger. I couldn't control the ultimate outcome of events—I couldn't save Duke's life, or my parents' marriage. And maybe life itself is nothing more than a bunch of moments strung together, a collection of highs and lows that only has the meaning we attach to it.

But where does forgiveness come from? If not from knowledge, then where?

Molly paused from her entry. And suddenly, she realized that if memorials were for the living, she needed to walk among the Californian members of them one last time before she left for Texas, to let the Dawn Patrol know what they had meant to her. She put her computer on standby and left the room.

As the surfers paddled out for the memorial, Archie waited at the tideline for AJ, Flea, Buzz Waldo, Riki, and Kai, who wandered down to the ocean in a group. Stuck in the sand beside him was an interesting collection of Duke's boards, which Archie assigned to the Dawn Patrol for the paddle-out. AJ got the busted-up "grandfather board," Riki a brand-new Spyder, Kai a long board Duke had surfed on in Hawaii.

"It was funny. There was one board I couldn't find back at his trailer, one I remembered from back in the day. Hard to forget. It was painted in total psychedelic colors."

"That board's spoken for," Kai said, smiling, when he saw the owner of that board at the top of the pier.

Molly waved at the group standing on the shore and ran through the sand, the last to arrive. "I'm sorry I'm late," she said.

"I'm glad you came," Kai said.

As the others splashed into the water, Molly lingered on the sand with Kai.

"What made you change your mind?" he asked.

"I had this silly idea that it might make you feel better if I came," she said.

"Not so silly."

"Look, I'd tell you that it wasn't your job to take care of Duke, but it wouldn't do any good. Because your sense of responsibility—even when it's misplaced—is what makes you who you are."

"You make me sound a little self-righteous," Kai said.

"Well, there *is* that element to it."

"You wound me, Molly," he said, only half teasing.

"Truth often does," Molly quipped, then added, "which is why I found lying so appealing."

They shared a smile. Kai picked up his board and paused before launching it into the water. "Do you believe Archie's version of what happened?"

"I have my doubts."

"Me too," he said.

"But I think we should make it the official version. "

"Why?"

"Because it's the kind of story Duke would have loved to tell."

Kai straightened and shook the hair off his face. It may

have been her imagination, but it seemed to Molly that he stood a little taller now, as if some of the burden of responsibility had fallen off his shoulders, and he was no longer weighted down by guilt.

Kai straightened and shook the hair off his face. It may have been her imagination, but it seemed to Molly that he stood a little taller now, as if some of the burden of responsibility had fallen off his shoulders, and he was no longer weighted down by guilt.

"Thanks, Molly. I don't know why, but that makes me feel better."

They paddled out way beyond the break, where they were joined by dozens more watermen and women who arrived by kayak, sailboat, and harbor patrol. The surfers straddled their boards, forming three concentric circles, holding hands to keep the circles tight. The boats idled on the outside. Molly pulled up in between Kai and Riki. The service began with testimonials. In no particular order, some offered stories, others remembrances, one a poem. And after they had finished, Archie pulled the box of ashes from his knapsack and said a simple prayer: "From water we are born. With water we live. And to the water we return. That by water we may know."

They all called out Duke's name three times in unison, sending up a roar, a plea to the ruler of the sea to embrace this lost soul. Many threw leis and flowers into the center of the circle. Archie emptied the box, spreading Duke's ashes across the stretch of water he had loved so much. A stream exploding from the jet sprays on the harbor patrol boats sent four arcs of water above the surfers, colliding with the mist in a dance of waters. With hoots and hollers, the surfers said their good-byes to a surfing legend, a man who had found peace in this lineup he called home.

Against the whirring of boat engines, the surfers at the memorial started back to shore. "Are you coming back in with us?" Kai asked Molly, who shook her head. She wasn't ready to leave the water yet. She needed some time alone. So as the others swam, paddled, and surfed the break, she turned her back on the land and faced the horizon, which was barely evident, sky melded into ocean in a seamless expanse of gray. She straddled her board and kept an eye on the approaching swells as she let the emotions of the day wash over like the fine mist from the fog.

Molly could smell the whale before she actually caught sight of him. The ancient barnacles on his face filled the air with a pungent odor, a musty fragrance eons old, wafting toward her from the beginning of time. It was the smell of the earth emanating from a creature who had never stepped on soil. She turned toward the scent just as the mottled Gray pushed himself out of the water vertically only twenty feet away and stared at her with a look of knowledge that pierced her very soul.

Duke said getting barreled was the closest he ever got to looking into the face of God. Well, I saw the eye of God in the eye of that whale. I thought if I knew what happened, I could forgive Duke. But knowing why someone did something doesn't make it hurt any less. No, forgiveness comes from a holy place, from connecting to the goodness or the divine or whatever you want to call it that lives inside all of us and that was certainly present in the whale that appeared before me. In the end, it's not how we die but how we live that's important. And I knew that Kai was right, that we had made a difference to Duke and to each other.

She washed up on the shore and shook the water off her head. A peace descended upon her like she had never felt before. She imagined the anger she carried for so long, unraveling like a ball of seaweed, twisted, ravaged, and decaying on the shore. For just a moment, she stopped being mad. And in the empty space left inside, a feeling of belonging swelled in its place. She mentally composed her next blog.

The water runs through us, they said. Well, the water runs through me, too.

She had never been so certain of anything in her life.

She didn't have to move back to Texas to heal. She had found a place that felt like home. Here in this place where land ends.

She shaded her eyes and watched a beautiful set form on the horizon. Up the hill in her room were bags waiting to be unpacked. On her bed was her open laptop and a new blog to begin. In Hermosa were people to tell of her decision to stay. But the magical spell of one more ride pulled her toward the water. The siren's call of a south-facing break was a potent aphrodisiac. She grabbed her board and like the sea lion heading for home, she returned to the ocean. And she never once looked back.

Karol Ann Hoeffner works as a screenwriter in Hollywood, having written original movies as well as novel adaptations for television miniseries and movies-of-the-week. Her first young adult novel, *All You've Got*, is based on her screenplay for the DVD, which was released by MTV in 2006. She is married with two children, one dog, and a cat, and lives quite happily at the beach.